ONE

Luke's mind drifted away from the episode of *Top Gear* he was watching on his iPad in bed. He yawned, tired after a full day of smiling and being jolly. His new job working as Santa in a grotto at the out-of-town mall near where he lived was surprisingly exhausting. Dealing with people in general all day was one thing, but interacting with small children was quite another. Roll on Christmas when he could hang up his Santa suit for good.

Bored and mildly horny, Luke picked up his phone and scrolled idly down the list of usernames and profile photos on Grindr.

He sighed as he saw all the conversations that had dwindled and died. Guys who only wanted to chat when they were horny, and never wanted to meet in person. Or guys who wanted to meet and have no-strings sex, but were "discreet." Everyone knew that was hook-up app code for married or cheating on a boyfriend—or girlfriend. Luke wasn't into that. Was it really too much to ask to find a single bloke who was actually interested in more than just a hook up?

It seemed that way, because Luke had been using the app for a year now and he still hadn't managed to find one. Disillusioned and fed up, he'd nearly deleted the app several times in the last month or so. Yet something kept him coming back, because potential boyfriends didn't grow on trees. Luke kept hoping that eventually Mr Right, or at least Mr Good Enough For Now, would come along.

He went through the list of chats, deleting a few conversations he'd given up on. Then he went back to the grid and refreshed it and started to scroll to see if there was anyone who looked interesting.

Luke paused on the profile shot of a slim, smooth chest, with a happy trail leading down to low-slung jeans. The username was Geek Guy and he was four miles away.

Geek Guy must be new, unless he'd changed his pic or his username. Luke would definitely have noticed him, because he had a thing for geeks, and he also liked skinny, twinky guys. He opened Geek Guy's profile to see if it gave much info.

New here, please be gentle, was all it said at the top.

5'10", twenty-nine years old—the same as Luke—slim build, vers bottom. Luke was a versatile top so Geek Guy sounded ideal. His profile said he was looking for mates, dates, and relationships. No mention of hook ups/no strings.

Ever hopeful that this next guy might be The One, Luke shot off a quick message. He always tried to go with something more than the usual "Hey."

Get Lucky: Hey, how are you? Welcome to the place where self-esteem comes to die.

A reply came back almost immediately.

Geek Guy: Well that's cheerful.

Get Lucky: LOL sorry. I forgot I was supposed to be

SECRET SANTA

JAY NORTHCOTE

COPYRIGHT

Warning

This book contains material that is intended for a mature, adult audience. It
contains graphic language, explicit sexual content, and adult situations.

*gentle. You caught me on a cynical day. Let's start over...
Hey, how are you?*

Geek Guy: I'm good thanks, how are you?

*Get Lucky: This is where the reply is usually "horny"
FYI.* Luke snorted at his own joke. It was true though.

Geek Guy: Haha. And are you?

*Get Lucky: A bit. So Geek Guy, can I see a pic of
your face?*

Geek Guy: Um, yeah sure. Let me find one.

Luke sent his own face pic. It was his favourite selfie
because he'd managed to smile without looking like a
complete twat. He'd recently trimmed his beard, and had
been having a good hair day. Luke wasn't under any illusions about his attractiveness. His profile shot was of his
torso, his chest was hairy, and his build was more "average"
than "toned." He was definitely more boy-next-door than
cover model.

He waited. There was no reply for several minutes, and
he was starting to wonder if Geek Guy had changed his
mind after seeing Luke's face. Or maybe he was talking to
someone else who sounded more interesting in another
chat.

Luke was about to give up and go back to watching *Top
Gear* when a photo appeared.

Wow.

Geek Guy's face was as pretty as his torso. He was
clean-shaven, with light brown hair, and hazel eyes. A
sweet, slightly shy smile curved plush pink lips that made
Luke's mind go to sexy places.

Get Lucky: Thanks. You're hot.

*Geek Guy: Sorry it took a while. I got distracted. And
thanks. You're hot too.*

Get Lucky: I guess. If you like hairy guys who don't work out ;)

Geek Guy: Jocks make me feel inadequate, and I love hairy chests.

Get Lucky: Cool.

Wanting to keep the conversation going, Luke quickly added: *So, where do you live?*

Geek Guy: Broad Leaze. You?

That was a suburb on the northern edge of the city, a little further out than Luke who lived east of the centre.

Get Lucky: Eastminster. Not too far away then.

As Luke tried to think where to steer the conversation next, Geek Guy beat him to it. That was a good sign; he was obviously keen to keep the chat going.

Geek Guy: What do you do for work?

Luke groaned. It was a sore subject at the moment. He'd been made redundant from his job at a mobile phone company recently and had been doing whatever temp jobs he could get to pay the bills for the last couple of months. His current job was the worst yet. No way was he going to tell a guy he was trying to impress that he spent his days dressed as Santa, so snotty brats could pull his beard while their proud parents took a million photos waiting for their hell-spawn to smile for the camera.

At least there was light at the end of the tunnel, because he had been offered a permanent job as a trainee pharmacy adviser starting in January. That couldn't come soon enough as far as Luke was concerned. He decided to be vague on the details.

Get Lucky: I work in retail. How about you?

Geek Guy: Yeah, similar. Retail, but IT related.

Get Lucky: Hence the username?

Geek Guy: Yeah :)

There was a pause in the conversation then. Luke was so used to this now it was like following a script. Well... one of two scripts. You either had the chat where the answer to "how are you?" was "horny" which usually ended in dick pics and jerking off. Or you had the conversations like this one where you skirted around getting to know each other a bit before finally getting to the nitty gritty.

Being the experienced one here, Luke decided to take it to the next level.

Get Lucky: S*o, what are you looking for on here?*

Geek Guy: *Other than the annihilation of my self-esteem?* ;)

Luke snorted. This guy was quick and funny. He liked that.

Get Lucky: *Yep.*

Geek Guy: *I don't know. A boyfriend is the ultimate goal I suppose. But mates or dates for starters.*

His honesty was refreshing. Luke smiled. He could count on one hand the amount of times he'd had a guy say that on here. Most of them were looking for a quick fuck, and if they were looking for more they were reluctant to admit it. They were too busy playing it cool and trying not to look needy.

Lost in thought, Luke suddenly remembered it was his turn to say something. He had nothing to lose, so thought he'd be up front. He knew from experience that if he wanted to meet a guy it was best to ask early on. Otherwise you often ended up chatting to someone for weeks, only to have him disappear into cyberspace.

Get Lucky: *So, are you interested in meeting for coffee or a drink? Chatting on here is fun, but the only way to tell if there's chemistry is to meet in person.*

There was a pause, just long enough to make Luke's heart sink. But then a new message flashed up.

Geek Guy: Yeah. Why not.

Get Lucky: So, when are you free? Evenings are best for me.

Luke's current job was nine to six, six days a week. He got Monday off, when some other poor sod got to stand in for him. The pay wasn't bad though, and the extra day each week meant he was earning more than in his last temp job in an office.

Geek Guy: Some evenings I work late, but not all.

Get Lucky: Got any free evenings this week?

He waited a minute or so, but Geek Guy had gone quiet. Hoping he hadn't scared him away, Luke added: *Sorry. Am I being too keen? I don't mean to be pushy.*

Geek Guy: No, no. It's fine. I was actually just checking my work schedule.

Luke grinned, excitement starting to build at the prospect of an actual date. It had been a few weeks since he'd met a guy in person, and that one had been disappointing. They'd blown each other, but hadn't really clicked so hadn't kept in touch after.

Geek Guy: I can probably do Thursday evening if that's any good?

Get Lucky: Yeah, that's fine. Coffee? Beers? And what time?

Geek Guy: Um. Coffee? I can be free around half six depending where.

Get Lucky: Is Starbucks at Lakeview Centre okay for you? It wasn't very exciting as a venue, but as it was where he worked, Luke could easily get there in time. And it wasn't too far from where Geek Guy lived and was easy to get to by car or public transport, so it should be convenient for him as well.

Geek Guy: Yeah, that's perfect.

Get Lucky: :)

Geek Guy: Sorry I've got to go now. It was nice talking to you, and I'll see you on Thursday.

Get Lucky: Good night. Oh, what's your name by the way? I'm Luke.

Geek Guy: I'm Theo. Night.

Luke scrolled back to look at the face pic Theo had sent. He smiled, eternal optimism burning bright again. Maybe this time it would lead to something better. Roll on Thursday. It was only a couple of days away.

TWO

"Daddy!" Archie wailed from the next room. Theo left his phone on his bed and hurried through to Archie's bedroom.

The soft glow of the nightlight lit Theo's path as he picked his way through the obstacle course of wooden train tracks, plastic dinosaurs, and Lego that Archie had been playing with while he was supposed to be in bed. Theo turned a blind eye to Archie getting up and playing, because he always got bored eventually, and was good at getting back into his bed and sleeping when he finally got tired.

Now Archie was four, it was rare for him to wake once he was down for the night, but it still happened occasionally —usually if he had a nightmare—and now he was sitting up in bed crying. He held his arms out when he saw Theo, and Theo scooped him up and sat with him in his lap. He kissed his sleep-warm cheek and rubbed his back, rocking instinctively as he soothed him.

"What's up, dude? Bad dream?"

"T-rex with big teeth." Archie sniffed, voice wobbly, "Chasing me."

"It's okay. There's no T-rex here. It was just a dream." Theo kept his voice calm and reassuring.

Another sob, but Archie was calming down now, already getting heavy in Theo's arms as he relaxed. He took a shaky breath. "Gone now?"

"All gone." Theo breathed in the scent of Archie's hair. Baby shampoo from his bath earlier and a hint of laundry detergent, with the unique Archie smell beneath the layers.

Archie brought his thumb up to his mouth now, cuddling the ragged old bit of cot blanket from when he was a baby that he still slept with every night.

Theo kept hold of Archie until his small body had gone floppy with sleep, then he carefully laid him back down in his bed and pulled up the covers. He pressed a soft kiss to his forehead and crept out again, stifling a curse as he stepped on a Lego brick.

Back in his own bedroom, Theo unlocked his phone and opened Grindr again. Get Lucky, or Luke as he now needed to think of him, had gone offline. Theo scrolled back through the conversation, pausing to look at the face of the guy he'd be meeting the day after tomorrow. He was cute. Theo liked guys with beards as long as they weren't too bushy. Luke's was neatly trimmed, dark like his short spiky hair. He had a nice smile, and lovely blue eyes. Theo hoped he'd find him as attractive in person.

His stomach swooped with nerves at the thought of a date. How long had it been since he'd gone on a date with a guy? He hadn't been on many since Archie was born, that was for sure. It wasn't because Archie was with him all the time; Theo only had him about half the week. But that, along with work, had been all-consuming for the last four years. Babies were exhausting with night feeds, and toddlers were equally tiring with the 5:00 a.m. starts to the day. On the rare night Theo had had the time or energy to do anything, he'd usually hung out with friends. Apart from one unsuccessful and all-too-brief relationship with a guy who'd slipped Theo his number at work one day—and who had disappeared like smoke when he found out that Theo had a kid—Theo had been single most of the time since Archie was born. Dating took too much effort. The occasional hook up in a bar had usually been all he could handle.

Now Archie was sleeping a little longer, and Theo was adapting to life as a part-time parent, he felt ready for more. He was lonely, and wanted someone to spend time with—not just for sex. His best friend, Paul, and his boyfriend, Jolyon, had met on Grindr nine months ago and were sickeningly happy. After a few beers last week, they'd managed to convince Theo to set up a profile. But he hadn't got around to it until tonight.

Another message notification flashed up in the app. It was from someone new, and he clicked on it to see a "Hey."

Theo was ready to sleep now, but didn't want to be rude and ignore, so he replied with a "Hi, how are you?"

He got a dick pic in reply, and the word "Horny."

Laughing, he remembered his conversation with Luke. It was a nice dick, but Theo wasn't in the mood to sext with a random stranger. He typed in a quick reply:

Geek Guy: Sorry man, long day. I'm just on my way to bed. Have fun.

Then he closed the app, turned the sound off on his phone, and settled down to sleep.

ON WEDNESDAY MORNING, Theo dropped Archie off at nursery with his overnight bag ready to go to Caroline's that night. They'd never lived together. Archie was a happy accident, the result of a drunken experiment between two friends. They were both committed parents and managed to have a fairly regular schedule for shared childcare, despite the fact that Caroline worked shifts as a nurse. It helped that Theo did regular fixed shifts at the Apple Store, and Caroline's mum helped out occasionally by having Archie if Caroline was working. Theo usually had him on Mondays, Tuesdays, and Saturdays, and Caroline had him the rest of the time.

He crouched down and gave Archie a hug and a kiss. "Have fun with Mummy, dude. And I'll see you on Saturday."

Saturday was one of Theo's days off, so he got to spend the whole day with Archie.

"Can we go on the train again?" Archie asked as Theo drew back.

"Train? Oh." Theo realised Archie was talking about the road train that went from one end of the shopping mall to the other. Theo had taken Archie to ride on it last weekend when it was pouring with rain, and they needed something to do. "I don't think so buddy. I was hoping we could do something outdoors this week."

"No! Train!" Archie's face crumpled and his blue eyes filled with tears.

"Okay, sure. We can go on the train again." Hopefully Archie would have forgotten all about it by Saturday and Theo could take him to the park instead.

Mollified, Archie beamed. "I like the train. Choo-choo!"

Theo chuckled. "I know you do." He ruffled his son's hair. "Okay, Archie. I've got to go. Have a fun day. I love you. Now why don't you go and play with the trains at nursery. Look, they've got them set up over there." He kissed

Archie's chubby cheek and pointed to a table in the corner where a couple of kids were studiously pushing carriages along a train track.

His attention caught, Archie happily trotted off to play.

IT WAS a busy day in work for Theo. With Christmas approaching, they were getting more and more people coming into the Apple Store for gift advice. Theo was glad he worked on the technical side of things rather than on the shop floor. But he still had a full schedule of people coming in for repairs and various issues with their devices.

He hardly had time to think about the fact he had a date tomorrow until he got to the end of his shift and checked his phone to find a Grindr notification. Opening it, he smiled when he saw it was from Luke, and then felt a little bad when he realised it had been sent a few hours ago.

Get Lucky: Hi, how are you today?

Theo saw that Luke was online, so he replied immediately.

Geek Guy: I was madly busy at work. But I'm done for the day now.

Get Lucky: Got plans for the evening?

Geek Guy: Not much. Just going home and chilling. I'm heading home now. How about you?

Get Lucky: I'm home now. Was going to go to my sister's for dinner but she cancelled because she's not feeling well.

Geek Guy: Aw. Shame.

Get Lucky: Yeah... but my niece and nephew would have climbed all over me and I'm not sure I have the energy to deal today.

Theo smiled. He knew the feeling. Not that he had a choice in dealing with Archie.

Geek Guy: Aw. How old are they?

Get Lucky: Two and four. I don't know how she copes with them.

Geek Guy: At least you get to give them back at the end of the day ;)

Get Lucky: Yeah. Luckily I'm not likely to have any of my own LOL.

Those words were like a punch in Theo's gut. He wasn't sure how to reply to that. So he shut the app and pocketed his phone instead.

Luke wasn't keen on kids then. That sucked, and not in the fun way. Suddenly Theo felt less excited at the prospect of their date. Archie was a huge part of Theo's life and Theo was looking for a boyfriend, not a hook up. What was the point of dating another guy who would probably run a mile when he found out that Theo had a kid who lived with him half the week?

He knew it was an overreaction because one date was unlikely to turn into anything serious anyway, so he should go and enjoy it for what it was. But Luke's throwaway comment had taken some of the shine off for Theo. It was a brutal reminder that his dating options were limited, as well as his time.

Still brooding as he parked his car on the street in front of his flat, Theo's phone buzzed with another Grindr notification. When he opened it, it was an unsolicited dick pic. He deleted without replying. Fuck that.

In his cluttered kitchen, Theo popped some frozen supermarket lasagne in the microwave, and put on a load of laundry while he was waiting for it to cook. Once he'd eaten, he lay on the sofa and watched some sci-fi drama on Netflix for a while.

His phone pinged again, and it was Luke this time.

Get Lucky: Make it home okay?

Theo sighed. He should be glad that Luke was making the effort to message, but he still felt a niggle of disappointment about Luke's child-related comment earlier.

Geek Guy: Yeah. Vegging on the sofa with Netflix now. How's your evening?

Get Lucky: Boring. I went to the gym earlier, and then ruined it by eating my weight in mac and cheese when I got home.

Geek Guy: Well, at least you made it to the gym. More than I ever manage.

Get Lucky: You not into fitness then?

Geek Guy: I run occasionally. But I've got out of the habit this winter. Should start again.

There was a short pause, before another message appeared.

Get Lucky: So, you still on for tomorrow night?

Theo stared at the message bubble. Was he? He liked what he'd seen of Luke so far. It would be daft to cancel on him just because he didn't want kids. Even though he might not be long-term boyfriend material, they could still hang out and have some fun for a while. Theo was probably over-thinking things as usual.

While he was debating, another message notification appeared at the top of the screen. It was from a profile that didn't have a photo at all. He opened the message anyway.

Top U Now: You free to fuck tonight?

Theo rolled his eyes and replied: *Not interested in NSA.*

No strings wasn't his cup of tea. Theo wanted some strings. And this was exactly why he should keep the date with Luke who seemed to be interested in more than a quick shag. Going back to their chat he typed quickly before he could change his mind and bail.

Geek Guy: Yeah, sure. Looking forward to it.

Get Lucky: Me too :) You wanna swap phone numbers and we can switch to WhatsApp or texting?

Geek Guy: Yes, definitely.

Get Lucky: Cool. Then I won't get inundated with other messages on here when I'm chatting to you.

Geek Guy? You too, huh?

Get Lucky: Goes with the territory. Here's my number…

Theo copied it into his contacts, then opened WhatsApp and sent Luke a message from there instead.

Theo: Hi, it's me.

Luke: Hey. Cute profile picture here. Living up to your Grindr name.

Theo was only slightly short-sighted, so he didn't wear his glasses much of the time. But his profile pic here was one he liked. His light brown hair was messy and the thick frames of his glasses emphasised the clear hazel of his eyes.

Theo: I guess so. Thanks :)

Luke's profile photo was the same face pic he'd sent Theo on Grindr.

Luke: So what are you watching on Netflix?

They spent the rest of the evening chatting intermittently about TV, movies, and books. They seemed to like some similar things: Sci-fi, Marvel, and crime drama. But Theo teased Luke for his love of *Top Gear*, and Luke took the piss out of Theo for his love of *The Great British Bake Off*. When Theo started to doze off over his phone, he made his excuses, and took himself to bed.

NEARING the end of another busy shift on Thursday,

Theo was too keyed up about his date to feel tired. He got out his phone to check the time—half five—and saw that he had a missed call, voice mail, and a text message from Caroline.

The text message said: *Urgent! Can you have Archie tonight? He's got a tummy bug and I don't want mum to have him in case she catches it, and I need to be at work by eight.*

"Shit," Theo muttered.

"You okay?" Nasreen, one of his co-workers, asked.

"Yeah, but I need to make an urgent call. Can you cover for me if my five-thirty appointment shows? I'll be as quick as I can."

He hit "call" as he headed out to stand just outside the front of the store. Caroline answered after a couple of rings.

"Oh good. You got my message at last. I was about to call the shop and try and get a message to you that way."

"Yeah, sorry. The sound was off."

"Of course." She sounded breathless and harassed. "So, Archie got sent home from nursery at lunchtime with a stomach bug. He's been throwing up all afternoon. Mum said she'd still have him, but I'd really rather you had him if you can?"

"Yes, of course," Theo answered immediately. Sue, Caroline's mum, had diabetes and it was best for her to avoid sick bugs if she could. She did so much for them already, mopping up Archie's vomit all night was beyond the call of grandparent duty. "What time shall I pick him up?"

"Can you get here by seven-thirty?"

"Sure."

"Okay, see you then."

"Bye." Theo hurried back to the tech desk at the back of the store.

"Everything all right?" Nasreen asked.

"Yeah. Archie's sick, but it's nothing major. Just means I need to have him tonight instead of his gran."

"Aw, poor kid. Hope you didn't have plans?"

"Oh bollocks." Focused on his parental responsibility, Theo had momentarily forgotten about his date with Luke. "Yes, I did. I'll have to rain check." He got out his phone, ready to message Luke. The sooner he could let him know the better; they were supposed to be meeting in less than an hour. But his next customer arrived before he managed to type the message. Putting his phone back in his pocket, he pasted on his best professional smile and introduced himself.

"Hi, I'm Theo. What seems to be the problem?"

THREE

"I don't think this is going to work," Luke said as the little girl on his knee wriggled, trying to get down, chubby arms reaching out for her mother.

"Come on, Lottie, smile for Mummy!" The mother grinned manically and waved, trying to distract her daughter. "Santa won't bring more presents for your stocking unless you're a good girl. I just want to get a photo so we can show Daddy who you met today."

That only made Lottie burst into tears. Luke couldn't blame her. He wasn't a parent, but even he could see that threatening a kid with no presents probably wasn't going to make them smile.

Lottie's mum obviously realised her mistake because she gave up at that point. She put her phone away and scooped up her crying child to comfort her. "Never mind, baby. Mummy was only being silly. Of course he'll bring you presents."

Lottie eyed Luke suspiciously from the safety of her mum's arms. "Lottie get pwesents?"

"Yes. Lots of presents," Luke said, trying to smile as

kindly as he could, which was difficult given that he had a giant beard covering most of his face. "And here's one now to take away with you." He got one of the random gifts out of the sack under the Christmas tree next to him and held it out.

Lottie looked as though she thought it might bite or electrocute her, so her mum took it instead. "There you are. What do you say?" she asked Lottie.

"Bye bye," Lottie said.

Luke burst out laughing. "Bye, Lottie."

"Thank you, Santa," the mum said.

Once they were gone, Luke breathed a sigh of relief. That was the last child of the day. He was free to go—and meet Theo.

He got up and hurried out of his grotto, closed the gate that led through the archway, and then put the sign on it that said: *Santa is off-duty now. Come back tomorrow between 9 and 6.*

In the staff changing room, he found Jamie, his elf assistant who helped manage the queue of parents and kids. Already out of his ludicrous costume of stripy tights and green knickerbockers, Jamie was down to purple boxers that clung to his pert little arse like paint. Luke couldn't help admiring it as Jamie bent to step into his skinny jeans. Jamie wouldn't mind, but his big beefy boyfriend, Marcus, might. Jamie had shown Luke a photo of him, and he looked like he could snap Luke in half with one hand.

"Was it just me, or did today feel longer than usual?" Luke asked as he started to get out of his Santa suit.

"Every day feels like a long day to me," Jamie said, pulling his T-shirt on, and then trying to spike up his peroxide-blond hair with his fingers with limited success. A day in the elf hat had taken its toll. "Thank God that's another one over. You got plans this evening?"

"I have actually," Luke said with a smile. "I've got a date."

"Ooh, awesome. Is he cute?"

"Yeah. Well... I think so. This will be our first meeting."

"I hope it goes well," Jamie said. "I'm seeing Marcus tonight. I can't wait. It's been a couple of days and I'm so horny."

Luke chuckled. "Have fun."

"Oh I will." Jamie gave him a wicked grin. "You too. See you tomorrow."

With nerves and excitement starting to flutter in his belly, Luke folded his Santa suit and put it away in his locker ready for tomorrow, and then put on the clothes he'd picked out that morning. It was only a coffee date but he wanted to make a good impression, so he'd gone with a button down and his nicest jeans instead of his usual T-shirt and hoodie for travelling to and from work.

By quarter past six, Luke was on his way to the Starbucks where they'd arranged to meet when his phone chimed with a WhatsApp notification. He stopped to read it, the flow of busy shoppers pouring around him as he read.

Theo: Sorry to cancel at short notice. Something came up and I can't make it.

The butterflies in Luke's stomach were abruptly wiped out by a flood of disappointment. He read the words again, trying to judge how genuine Theo sounded. The message was short and didn't give much away, and there was no suggestion that they should reschedule. Luke wanted to be optimistic. But he'd been stood up before, and usually assumed that the guy had got a better offer, or had changed his mind about wanting to meet. Not quite ready to give up hope, he typed:

Aw. That's a shame, but no worries. Hope everything's okay? He thought about suggesting they rearrange, but then decided that should be up to Theo so he pressed "send."

Theo replied immediately with: *Yeah. Thanks.*

Well that didn't make things any clearer. Trying not to read too much into Theo's curt response, Luke sighed, pocketed his phone, and went to catch his bus home instead.

NOT WANTING a lonely night in front of his iPad again, Luke was glad to find his flatmate, Charlie, was in when he got home. She was lying on the sofa with a blanket over her knees and a cup of tea and a Kindle in her hands.

"Hey, Luke," she said. "How was your day?"

"Not the best." Luke sighed.

"What's up?" Charlie put her Kindle down and met his gaze.

"Dating woes. You know I was supposed to be meeting that guy, Theo? Well he cancelled on me right at the eleventh hour."

"Oh, that sucks. I'm sorry."

"Are you busy tonight?"

"Well I had thrilling plans to binge watch *Supernatural* and swoon over Sam and Dean until I pass out, so I guess that's a no. Why?"

Luke grinned despite his shitty mood. "Because I need moderate amounts of alcohol and copious amounts of junk food. Do you wanna join me?"

"Well, how can I refuse an offer like that? What kind of junk food?"

"We could order pizza?" Luke suggested.

"Sounds perfect. And I have a bottle of Pinot Grigio, and a bucket of chocolate brownie ice cream I bought on my way home from work."

"You're the best," Luke said. "I'll pay for the pizza then."

ONE GIANT CHICKEN and bacon pizza and a bottle of wine later, they were passing the tub of ice cream back and forth between them. It was melting at the edges, and Luke was starting to feel a bit sick. Drowning his misery with alcohol and junk food was like sticking a plaster on an infected cut. It masked it temporarily, but only made it fester under the surface till it came spilling out again.

"No thanks," he said as Charlie offered him the tub again. "I'm done."

"Yeah." She took the spoon out and licked it clean. "Me too I think."

"I'll put it back in the freezer."

Luke picked it up along with the pizza box and carried them through to the kitchen.

When he got back, he flopped down on the sofa, and sighed heavily. His thoughts turned to Theo, and he got out his phone in case he'd missed a message. But the lock screen was empty of notifications.

"Should I message him again? Or would that be too pushy?"

"How did you leave it earlier?" Charlie asked, pausing the TV.

Luke showed her the messages from today.

"It's so hard to tell with texts." She frowned. "I mean, he might have a totally legit reason and have been busy dealing with whatever happened, or driving, or something."

"Surely he could have found the time to text again by now?"

She shrugged. "Technically it's your turn to reply. Maybe he's waiting for that."

That was a good point. Although Theo's last message had been super short, it was still a message. Standard texting rules applied.

"But what should I say?"

"Just ask him if he wants to rearrange. What have you got to lose?"

"Nothing apart from my pride I guess. Although that's in increasingly short supply thanks to dating."

Charlie groaned. "I know, tell me about it. I can remember how soul-destroying it is sometimes."

"Okay, okay. Don't rub it in." Luke rolled his eyes. Charlie had hung up her dating hat six months ago when she met a lovely guy through OkCupid. Unfortunately for Charlie, he was based a hundred miles away in London, so it was a long distance relationship for now. But they saw each other most weekends, and talked on the phone or Face-Time every day.

"Yeah. Sorry. I'm just saying I get it though. Dating apps are brutal. It sucks putting yourself out there over and over and getting knocked back. It's like you lose a little bit of your soul each time."

"Wow. That's cheerful. And also not helping."

She was right though. That was exactly how it felt. Each new online connection involved sharing part of yourself in the hopes of forging a relationship. Then when it came to nothing, Luke sometimes felt that he hadn't got all the pieces of himself back.

But what else was he going to do? It was hard meeting

people in his day-to-day life. He wasn't quite ready to give up on the dating and hook-up apps yet.

He sighed, preparing to chip off another sliver of his soul and send it to Theo. "Okay. I'll message him."

Luke decided to be up front. He didn't like playing games.

Luke: I was looking forward to meeting you today, so if you're still up for it do you want to rearrange? If you've changed your mind, just let me know.

He pressed "send" and watched the screen. WhatsApp showed him that the message had been delivered, but it wasn't read immediately.

Knowing he'd drive himself crazy watching his phone all night, he turned the sound off and handed his phone to Charlie.

"Here. Keep this until the end of the episode. Stop me checking it every thirty seconds."

She chuckled. "Okay then."

AS SOON AS the credits started to roll, Luke asked for his phone back.

There was still no reply from Theo, and another jolt of disappointment hit Luke in the gut.

He opened WhatsApp and felt ten times worse when he could see that his message had been read.

"Ugh. He read it twenty minutes ago but hasn't bothered to reply. That's not a good sign."

"Maybe he's busy?" Charlie's sympathetic face only made Luke feel worse.

"It doesn't take long to type something like: 'yes, okay. I'll get back to you.' Does it?"

"I suppose not. But don't give up yet. Give me your phone back and we'll watch another episode."

By midnight, Luke was dozing off. He reclaimed his phone from Charlie and braced himself as he checked it again. He wasn't even surprised this time to see that there was still nothing.

"Okay. I officially give up. I'm going to bed now."

"I'm sorry, honey," Charlie said. "And I know it's a cliché, but it really is his loss. You're awesome."

"Yeah, yeah. Thanks. And thanks for the company."

"Always." She got up and gave him the biggest bear hug she could manage—given that she was five-foot-two and built like a pixie. What she lacked in size she made up for in strength as she squeezed him tight.

FOUR

Theo drifted into wakefulness, wondering where the hell he was for a moment. The sound of the television was a clue, as was the crick in his neck, and he winced as he sat up, stretching his aching muscles and orienting himself.

Of course.

He was in his living room sleeping on the sofa. He'd intended to go to bed when Archie settled, but must have passed out exhausted. Checking his watch, Theo saw that it was seven in the morning. He groaned. Three hours' sleep wasn't enough to function on. Getting up, he walked quietly to Archie's room and crept in. Archie was fast asleep. Cheeks still a little pale, and his blond hair tousled, he lay on his back, arms spread wide, and the covers down to his waist. Theo carefully pulled the duvet up. Archie didn't stir. The poor kid must be shattered. He'd been up half the night either throwing up, or being cleaned by Theo. He'd vomited all over himself and the bed several times before he'd finally stopped puking and slept.

Theo went to put a load of washing in the dryer, and stuffed another set of Archie's bedding into the washing machine. Then he put the kettle on for some coffee. Excessive amounts of caffeine were the only way he was going to get through today. Clouded by exhaustion, he tried to work out a plan. He was on a late shift, so didn't have to rush. But there was no way Archie could go to nursery as he usually did. Caroline would have to take him and lose out on the sleep she'd desperately need after her night shift.

Once he had a mug of steaming coffee, Theo sat on the sofa with his phone and sent a quick text to Caroline to update her, and to ask if he could drop Archie with her on his way to work around midday. She'd still be working now, so he knew she wouldn't reply for a while. His gaze caught on the WhatsApp logo and he suddenly remembered he hadn't replied to Luke last night.

Opening the thread, he read the message again, feeling bad for forgetting. He'd been about to reply when Archie had thrown up again and by the time he'd changed the bed, and Archie, and put the sheets on to wash, it had completely gone out of his head. Poor Luke probably thought Theo was a total arsehole for reading and not replying. By now he'd probably assumed that Theo had blown him off and wasn't interested in meeting at all.

Am I?

Theo tried to think through the fog of tiredness that muddled his brain. He'd been looking forward to meeting Luke, despite his reservations after Luke's negative comment about kids. But after the night Theo had just had, it seemed crazy to be thinking about dating someone who had no desire to have children. Sure, they might hook up and have some fun, but if Theo was being honest, he wanted more than that. He wanted a relationship, and if Luke wasn't keen on kids it seemed unlikely it was ever going to work. Luke was cute though, and he seemed like a nice guy. Maybe it was still worth pursuing. After all, Theo was hardly likely to end up finding a long-term relationship right off the bat, and he had to start somewhere. If nothing else, Luke might be a warm-up round to get Theo back into the swing of dating.

Decision made, Theo sent: *Sorry I didn't reply last night. Things were a bit hectic. But I'd still like to meet.*

After drinking his coffee, Theo pottered around tidying up a bit and then lay down on the sofa in front of morning telly. His eyelids started to droop, and he was dozing off when he heard small feet shuffling into the room.

Theo opened his eyes to see Archie standing in front of him, his thumb in his mouth. He was dressed in a T-shirt and tracksuit bottoms because all his pyjamas were in the wash.

"Hey, little dude. Are you feeling better?" Theo asked. Archie looked better, with more colour in his cheeks now.

Archie nodded, then took his thumb out of his mouth long enough to say, "Want blankey."

Archie's blanket had been a casualty in one of the many vomiting incidents the night before.

"It's in the drier, let me go and find it for you." Theo heaved himself up, his body protesting.

When he came back, Archie had changed the channel to CBeebies, and stolen Theo's spot on the sofa. He reached for his blanket with grabby hands and snuggled down on the cushions.

"Are you hungry?" Theo asked.

Archie shook his head. So Theo went to get him some watered down apple juice in a sippy cup.

"Drink this, buddy. Your body probably needs it."

Theo was ready for breakfast now, so he made himself some toast while Archie watched TV. Then, as Archie seemed happy and didn't look as if he was going to throw up again, Theo risked having a quick shower.

When he came back to the living room, he refilled Archie's juice cup and then checked his phone. There was a missed call and a message from Caroline. The message just said: *Of course, that's fine. How is he now?*

Theo hit "call" rather than texting, she'd probably be on the bus home by now so should be able to speak. Sure enough she answered immediately.

"Hi," she said.

"Hey. So that was a fun night. Not. He seems okay this morning though."

"Oh God, was it bad? I'm sorry you got lumbered."

"It's fine. Goes with the territory. But it was pretty awful. Poor Archie was sick every couple of hours for most of the night. He seems okay this morning, though. Hasn't been sick since about 4:00 a.m., so I'm pretty sure he's over it now."

"Is he eating?"

"Not yet."

"Drinking?"

"Yes."

"Good." She sounded relieved. "Okay, my bus stop is coming up so I need to go. I'll see you later."

THEO STILL HADN'T HAD a reply from Luke by the time he dropped Archie off with Caroline. Mulling it over as he drove to work, he realised he was disappointed, despite his misgivings. He'd been hoping Luke would suggest some alternative days to meet. Maybe Theo should have done that?

Looking at the message thread again while sitting in his

car after he'd parked, he thought about doing that now. Would he look too pushy if he did that?

Ugh. Dating etiquette was difficult. It was impossible to work out what was going on in the other person's head.

Getting out of his car, Theo shivered. It was freezing today. Winter had well and truly arrived with a flurry of sleet carried by an icy wind that stung his cheeks. He hurried across the car park and in through the revolving doors of the huge out-of-town mall he worked in. Inside, it was already bustling with shoppers. Elaborate Christmas decorations hung from the high glass ceiling and the shop fronts competed with snow scenes, glitter, and fairy lights, trying to grab the attention of potential customers.

The Apple Store was sedate compared to most, only a few tasteful lights along the window as a nod to the season. Theo passed through the doors, greeting his colleagues as he walked through to the staff room at the back of the shop. He was only just on time, having got stuck in slow traffic for a while. He hurried to his locker to stash his coat and keys, switched his phone to silent, and went straight back out to start work.

WHEN IT WAS time for his break, Theo went to the nearest coffee shop to recaffeinate and get some food. He checked his phone while he was in the queue, and felt a flicker of excitement when he saw he had a WhatsApp message from Luke. But the content wasn't exactly thrilling.

Luke: That's okay :) Life happens.

The smiley face was a good sign, but the shortness wasn't. And Luke hadn't made any effort to set up another date. Theo decided he owed it to Luke to try as he was the one to cancel. Once he was sitting down with his coffee and a panini he sent Luke another message.

Theo: Do you want to try to find another time to meet?

He watched and saw that the message was delivered, but not read. Luke was probably working. Theo opened the Kindle app and read while he ate his lunch and drank his coffee. There was still no reply by the time he had to get back to work, and he turned the sound off on his phone again so it wouldn't ping while he was with customers.

THEO KEPT CHECKING his phone every time he had a spare minute. He had a text from Caroline letting him know that Archie had bounced back and was fine now, "way too full of energy and eating everything" was how she described it, which made Theo smile. That was good; he'd be able to enjoy his day with Archie tomorrow then. Technically he should probably keep Archie at home for the day given that he'd been sick on Thursday and into the small hours of Friday, but Archie had way too much energy to be cooped up all day. There was rain forecast though, so, the park probably wouldn't be an option. He remembered his promise to Archie to take him on the train at the shopping mall. That would be as good a plan as any.

When his shift ended at nine he still hadn't had a reply from Luke. Feeling despondent now, Theo drove home bug-eyed with exhaustion after his mostly sleepless night and the long day at work. He got home around half nine, and although he was hungry he was too tired to cook. So after getting into sweatpants he made a couple of pieces of toast and a mug of hot chocolate and curled up on the sofa under a blanket to watch TV.

Once his belly was full, Theo's eyes started to drift

closed and he'd just dozed off when his phone chimed with a WhatsApp alert. Jerking awake, Theo grabbed his phone.

Luke: Yes okay. When are you free?

Theo checked his schedule, and replied a few minutes later: *Wednesday or Friday evening next week are good for me.*

He waited, watching the screen for a moment. Luke had seen the message so Theo was hoping for an immediate reply. But he didn't get one. To kill some time, Theo went to brush his teeth and use the toilet, taking his phone with him. But still nothing.

Frustrated, Theo wondered if Luke was deliberately leaving him hanging. He huffed out a sigh. Dating was too much like hard work and he hadn't even been on a sodding date yet. Knackered and fed up, he wanted sleep more than anything right now. Knowing that he wouldn't sleep if he kept his phone on hand, he put it on silent and left it in the living room before heading to bed.

THE NEXT MORNING Theo was still fast asleep when his alarm went off at half eight. It wasn't much of a lie in considering it was his day off, but he had to go to pick up Archie at ten. He needed to tidy up and shower before then, and go grocery shopping on the way to Caroline's. He picked up his phone on his way through the living room to the kitchen, and saw that Luke had eventually replied to him last night—but not until nearly midnight when Theo had been out for the count.

Luke: I can do Wednesday.

Theo rolled his eyes as he put his phone down to fill the kettle and switch it on. It took him an hour and a half to reply with four words? Compared to their earlier interactions, their conversation was stilted and awkward now. It felt as though things were drifting, even though they were still trying to arrange a date.

Deciding to be pushy, Theo sent back: *Okay cool. Same time and place, half six at Starbucks? Second time lucky* :)

The reply pinged in almost immediately for a change.

Luke: Yes, that works for me.

Theo grinned. The date was back on.

Theo: Cool. I'll see you then.

Luke: Okay. I'm starting work soon, so have a good day.

Theo: Cheers. You too.

FIVE

Luke put his phone away with a smile on his face. After their frustrating game of message tag, he finally had another date with Theo lined up. He had deliberately been a little slow to reply last night, because he still wasn't sure how keen Theo was given how uncommunicative he'd been after he'd first cancelled. Luke didn't like playing games, but there was a fine line between being chatty, and be so keen that he scared guys away. Hopefully when they met, he'd be able to gauge Theo better, and would also know if he was worth pursuing.

"You look pleased with yourself," Jamie said. He had his back to Luke and was eyeing him in the mirror as he smeared red circles onto his cheeks with face paint.

"Yeah, just lined up another date with Theo—remember the guy I was supposed to meet last week but then he cancelled?"

"Oh, that's awesome."

"Yeah. Hopefully it will work out this time." Luke slipped on his Santa jacket and started doing up the buttons. "Hurry up with the mirror. I need to get my beard on."

IT WAS ONLY the second Saturday in December, and Luke's second weekend as Santa. But it was already significantly busier than the one before. They booked people in for an hour slot, and then had a numbered ticket system, so kids and parents could explore the outer part of the grotto while they waited. There were some toys and colouring activities to keep the kids entertained, as well as animatronic reindeer singing Christmas songs. Jamie had his work cut out keeping the queue moving and ushering the parents and kids in and out.

Luke dealt with all the usual issues. Kids who were scared of him, kids who wouldn't smile for their parents' camera phones, kids who wanted to pull his beard, and kids who just wanted to go back and see the reindeer instead of hanging out with Santa. There were some pretty cute ones too, Luke had to admit. He liked to grumble about how annoying children were, but they weren't all bad.

By lunchtime Luke was shattered, but a coffee and a sandwich recharged his Santa batteries for the afternoon. Back in his grotto, he was in the zone, running on adrenaline as the parents and kids kept coming.

He'd just finished with two little girls and their mum—who'd miraculously managed to get a photo with both of them on his knee, and both smiling at the same time—and braced himself ready for the next one. He got a tea break after this, only fifteen minutes, but he needed to pee and was looking forward to getting out of his seat for a while.

"Here we go, Archie," a male voice said. "Santa is in here. Look!"

Luke focused on the little boy first. He had straight blond hair and blue eyes that widened as he saw Luke. He stopped in the doorway, clutching his dad's hand tightly, a plastic dinosaur in his other hand. Getting used to dealing with the nervous kids now, Luke toned down his fake jolly Santa voice a little as he said, "Hello. How are you today? Archie is it?"

The little boy nodded. "Yes."

"Do you want to come and meet Santa, Archie?" the man asked.

Only then did Luke look at the man with Archie, and he recognised him instantly.

It was Theo. With light brown hair that glinted gold where the light caught it and fine features, he was just as cute in real life as he was in the photo Luke had seen. Theo wouldn't recognise Luke though, not with a giant white beard covering half his face, and now wasn't the time to introduce himself.

Was Archie Theo's son? He hadn't mentioned having a child, but then they hadn't chatted much yet, and Luke hadn't asked. With a jolt of unease, Luke wondered whether Theo was cheating on a wife or girlfriend. It happened a lot on Grindr. Luke always avoided any guys who made that clear on their profiles.

Still stuck in the doorway, Theo met Luke's gaze, and shrugged helplessly. "Sorry, he's a bit shy with strangers at the best of times. But I thought I'd give this a go."

Luke snapped back into Santa mode, deliberately ramping up his Santa act to disguise his voice. "That's okay. I have a present for you, Archie, if you'd like to come and say hello to me?"

"Is it a train?" Archie asked.

Taken by surprise at the direct question, Luke chuckled. "Probably not, I don't think my elves can make trains."

"I like trains," Archie said. He let go of Theo's hand now and approached cautiously. "I like dinosaurs too."

"Me too." Luke didn't really have strong feelings about trains, or dinosaurs, but he wanted to keep Archie talking.

"Daddy took me on a train."

"Oh yes?" Luke said, looking at Theo then.

"Yes, on the train here earlier," Theo clarified. Well that answered one of Luke's questions.

"How lovely. Was that fun?" Luke asked Archie who was standing close to him now.

Archie nodded. "Yes. But it was very slow."

Theo laughed. "Yeah, sorry, buddy. I'll take you on a faster one again soon."

"So, Archie. Are you being a good boy for your daddy today?"

"Yes," Archie said seriously. "So, can I have a present?"

"Of course. But does your daddy want to take a photo of you with me first?" Luke looked at Theo.

"That would be good wouldn't it, Archie? I think Mummy would like to see a photo of you with Santa."

Luke's stomach lurched. Desperate to dig for more information on how Archie's mum fitted into this equation, he asked, "Where is your mummy today?"

"She's at work," Archie said. "I'm sleeping at Daddy's today."

So they weren't together. Luke sighed in relief. "Do you want to sit on my knee for a photo?"

Archie seemed to have decided Santa was okay, because he said, "Okay."

Theo lifted him up, and Luke put an arm around Archie to keep him from slipping as Theo got out his phone.

"Are you ready? Smile, Archie!" Theo grinned at them in encouragement. He had a lovely smile.

Luke grinned back, and said, "Ho, ho, ho!" as Theo took a few shots.

"Okay?" Luke asked.

"Yeah, they came out well. Thanks."

Archie wriggled, so Luke let him jump down. "Can I have a present now?"

He was very articulate, Luke thought. He looked a similar age to Connor, Luke's nephew, so that would make him around four. But he spoke more clearly and precisely than Connor did.

"Say please, Archie," Theo said. "And it's more polite to wait until you're offered one."

"Please?" Archie met Luke's gaze with a hopeful expression.

"Absolutely." Luke reached for the sack by his chair and let Archie pick a present. They were all cuddly toys of various types, so Archie wasn't going to get the train he'd been hoping for.

"What do you say, Archie?" Theo said.

"Thank you," Archie said. "Bye bye." With the present clutched in his hands, he turned and rushed out through the archway.

"Wait for me!" Theo said, hurrying after him. "Thanks," he called back over his shoulder to Luke.

LUKE MESSAGED Theo that evening once he was home and relaxing on the sofa. Charlie was away visiting her boyfriend, so Luke had the flat to himself and free rein with the TV remote.

Luke: Hey, how are you. Did you have a good Saturday?

Having met Theo earlier, Luke was feeling all the more excited about their date next week. Theo was definitely attractive, and he seemed like a nice guy from what Luke had seen. Satisfied that Theo was single, and not cheating on Archie's mum, it didn't bother Luke that Theo had a kid, although it might make dating him a little more complicated.

He was relieved when Theo replied quickly.

Theo: Yes thanks. Busy but good. How about you?

Luke: I was working. Chilling out at home now.

Theo: Same :)

Theo: The chilling at home now part, that is. I had a day off today.

Luke: Nice. Did you do anything fun?

Theo: Not much. Just a bit of shopping, then pottering around at home.

No mention of Archie. Luke wondered whether to be honest and confess to his Santa alter ego? He didn't want to make things awkward, and it was up to Theo to share personal details about himself. Perhaps if Luke led the conversation in the right direction it would give Theo the opportunity to open up.

Luke: What are you up to the rest of the weekend? I'm working again tomorrow, but then I'm going to my sister's place for dinner.

Theo: I'm working tomorrow too. No plans apart from that.

Luke: Do you have family locally?

Theo: No. My parents live up North.

Luke frowned. It wasn't exactly a lie, depending on how Theo had interpreted the question. If he'd wanted to tell Luke about his son it would have been a good time for him to mention it. But maybe Theo would prefer to tell him face-to-face when they met. Luke decided to change the subject.

Luke: I need a new series to watch on Netflix, any recommendations?

Theo: What are you in the mood for?

Luke: Something a bit dark I think. Gripping.

Theo: How to Get Away With Murder *is good. Or* Dexter *if you haven't watched that yet.* Orphan Black?

Luke: Seen the first two. Might give Orphan Black *a go. Cheers. I'll try it this evening.*

Theo: Enjoy.

Luke: Thanks. Talk later, or tomorrow.

Theo: Okay :)

SIX

For the next few days, Theo exchanged occasional messages with Luke. Sometimes they'd chat back and forth a bit, but other times messages would go unanswered by one or both of them for a while—especially during the day when they were both busy with work.

Theo was assuming that their Wednesday date was still on, as he hadn't heard otherwise, and he didn't want to be paranoid and keep checking.

But on Wednesday morning when Luke sent his usual, "Good morning" message. Theo replied with: *So, are you still on for tonight?*

Luke replied immediately.

Luke: Yes, definitely. You?

Theo: Yes, unless anything drastic happens between now and then.

There weren't likely to be any Archie emergencies today. Caroline wasn't working tonight, so Archie would be at her place.

Luke: Let's hope it doesn't. If you cancelled a second time I might get paranoid.

Theo: I hope it doesn't either. I'd hate to make you paranoid.

Luke: :) See you at half six then. Gotta go now.

Theo smiled, heart lifting hopefully. He enjoyed chatting with Luke, and he really hoped it translated into them getting on in person.

FATE WAS on Theo's side. His day went smoothly and he finished work on time. Before he left, he changed out of his work T-shirt and put on a dark green plaid shirt instead. He was already wearing jeans and black boots, so with the work shirt swapped out for something casual he was ready to go. In the staff toilet he checked his hair in the mirror, running his hands through it to mess it up a little. Heart pounding harder with nerves, he gave his reflection a last look. He'd do.

As he walked out of the store, he sent Luke a quick message: *I'm on my way.*

His phone pinged as he was putting it in his pocket.

Luke: I'll be there in ten mins.

Theo: What do you want to drink?

Luke: Gingerbread latte please.

The date was definitely on.

Starbucks was busy as usual, and by the time Theo got through the queue to order and was waiting for their drinks, he was on high alert looking out for Luke. It was weird meeting someone when you'd only seen a picture of them. A photo was never the same as seeing someone in person. What if they didn't recognise each other?

"Gingerbread latte and a vanilla latte for Theo!" One of the baristas called.

Theo moved forward to get them, and then stopped to

get some stirrers and shove a couple of napkins into his pocket. Hands full, he edged his way carefully through the crowd of waiting people, concentrating on not bumping into anyone. He'd asked for the drinks in takeaway cups in case there wasn't space to sit down.

"Hi, you must be Theo," a deep voice said.

Looking up, Theo saw Luke. With short dark hair and the neat beard that Theo remembered from Luke's photo on Grindr, his blue eyes were fixed on Theo as he gave a slightly nervous smile.

"Yeah. Luke. Hi." Theo smiled, and Luke's grin widened, his expression relaxing.

They stared at each other dumbly for a moment.

"I forgot to ask if you're a handshake or a hug kind of guy," Luke said. "But as your hands are full I guess we have to run with the awkward hellos."

Theo chuckled. "Yeah. Unless you want to end up wearing your latte, that's probably for the best. Here." He handed Luke the cup in his left hand. "I think this one is yours. Shall we see if we can find somewhere to sit?"

"Sure."

The dating gods were kind to them, and an elderly couple at a table for two nearby were just getting up and leaving. So they swooped in to claim the spot. It was a tiny table squeezed into a corner, and their knees bumped under it.

"Sorry," Theo said, rearranging so they weren't touching anymore.

"It's okay. I don't mind." Luke took the lid off his cup and stirred it. "God, I need this. It's been a long day."

"Yeah mine too." Theo inhaled the scent of his coffee. Still too hot to drink, he wished he could get the caffeine into his system by breathing it in.

"Where do you work?"

"The Apple Store."

"Oh yes, I remember you said IT. Sales? Or the tech side?" Luke asked.

"Techy. I fix stuff."

"Do you nose around on people's phones while you're fixing them? I've always wondered. I don't think I'd be able to resist scrolling through their photos or search history."

Theo chuckled. "Not intentionally. But occasionally I've seen stuff they'd probably rather I didn't." He scooped up some of the foam with his finger, and licked it, noticing Luke's eyes track the movement before returning to meet his gaze. "So how about you, where do you work? Somewhere here too, I presume, as you said retail."

Luke looked down at his coffee, stirring it again. "Oh, um. I work in M&S at the moment. It's only temporary though. Just till Christmas. After that I'm starting at Lloyds-Pharmacy as a trainee pharmacy adviser."

Was it Theo's imagination, or was Luke blushing a little? "Oh cool. That sounds like it should be good. Bit of a career change?"

"Yeah. I hope so. Eventually I want to do a degree in pharmacy. I'm hoping I can do that part-time alongside working there. It will be good to be doing something with a long-term goal in mind." Luke glanced up, more animated now they were talking about his future plans.

"So do you do shift work at M&S? Must be busy there in the run-up to Christmas. Do you have to work evenings sometimes?"

"Um. Yeah, sometimes." Luke took a gulp of coffee and then winced. "Ow, fuck. I burned my tongue."

"Oh damn. I always forget how hot it is under the foam. Do you want some water?"

"Yes please."

Theo got a bottle out of his bag and handed it to Luke.

"Thanks." Luke took a gulp and held it in his mouth for a while, a pained expression on his face. When he eventually swallowed, he grinned sheepishly. "Way to make a good first impression, huh?"

Theo smiled back. Luke had really nice eyes. With his dark brows and lashes, the blue was intense. Theo felt his cheeks heat as he held Luke's gaze past the point of normal politeness. "You're not doing so badly."

"Yeah?" Luke's grin spread, dimpling his cheeks. "I'm glad to hear it. Neither are you."

Theo ducked his head, focusing on the coffee cup in his hands as his ears burned. The silence between them became awkward, and Theo didn't know what to say next. Salvation came in the form of the piped Christmas music as he tuned into Bing Crosby's "White Christmas," which was pouring out of a speaker nearby.

"What's your favourite Christmas song?" he asked.

Luke raised his eyebrows, but ran with the subject change. "Am I allowed to hate all of them?"

Theo snorted. "No. Favourites are all relative. Even if you hate them all, there must be some that you hate less. So therefore one of those must be your favourite."

"Ooh. Mr Logic." Luke's lips quirked in amusement. "Okay. Well, I guess 'Little Saint Nick' by the Beach Boys is okay."

"Oh yeah, that's a good one." Theo nodded his approval.

"How about you? What's your favourite?"

"I like 'Sleigh Ride,'" Theo said, and Luke grimaced. "What? I know it's one that gets played to death, but it's just so...." Theo tried to find the right words.

"Cheesy? Relentlessly jolly?" Luke offered.

"I'm on a date with the Grinch aren't I? Or maybe Scrooge. Do you hate Christmas in general, or just the music?"

Luke shrugged, eyes twinkling. "Eh. I like the turkey."

Theo sighed wistfully. "Yeah. I like Christmas dinner too."

Sadly, he probably wouldn't be getting one this year. He was gutted that he couldn't go home for Christmas. His parents lived in the northeast and it was too far to travel for a day. He couldn't go for longer unless he went alone, and he didn't want to be away from Archie for too long, plus he couldn't lumber Caroline with extra childcare. Christmas was going to be a lonely affair. Archie was with Caroline on Christmas Day, and they were going to her mum's. They'd invited Theo, but he'd declined. Caroline had a newish boyfriend, Daniel, who she seemed pretty serious about, and Theo didn't want to feel that he was stepping on anyone's toes. So he'd be spending Christmas Day alone, and then had Archie coming to him for Boxing Day when Caroline was working.

Last year, Theo had spent Christmas with his best mate, Paul. Paul didn't get on with his family, so had been glad of an excuse not to make a duty visit. They'd hung out, cooked dinner together, and drunk too much wine while watching all the Christmas specials on TV. But this year, Paul was going to Jolyon's family in London for Christmas. Theo was happy for him, really he was, but he couldn't help being a bit sad for himself. Christmas was a lonely time if you didn't have someone to spend it with.

Picking up his coffee, Theo took a sip. It was the perfect temperature now and the sweet warmth of his vanilla latte lifted his spirits again. He was on a date with a cute guy, and spending Christmas alone wasn't the worst thing in the world. At least there'd be loads of stuff to watch on telly. He gulped again, suddenly feeling hungry, and wishing he'd got something to eat as well as to drink.

"Is it cool enough to drink now?" Luke stuck a finger through his foam. "Oh yeah. I think I might be able to risk it without further injury." He sucked the foam off his finger while he held Theo's gaze.

"I think you got it all." Theo looked pointedly at the finger, still in Luke's mouth.

Luke dipped and sucked again, releasing his finger with a pop this time. "It's yummy though. The foam is the best bit." His grin was wicked. "What?" he said innocently as Theo raised his eyebrows.

"Nothing at all." Theo took another sip, watching Luke over the rim of his cup as Luke finally picked his up and drank. Luke's flirting had made non-coffee-related warmth pool in Theo's stomach, and somewhere a little south of there too. How long had it been since he'd had his dick sucked? It felt like forever. There had been that guy in the toilets at a club, but that was months ago, back in the summer, or even the spring. And Theo hadn't really been able to get into it because the lock on the cubicle door was broken and he'd been worried about someone walking in on them.

Suddenly a child's angry scream cut through Theo's thoughts. He whipped around to look and saw a couple at a nearby table with a little girl in a highchair. She was crying, her face red and furious as she struggled to get down. The mother was offering her a piece of her cake, speaking calmly, and trying to placate her. But the child dashed it out of the mother's hand onto the floor. Theo winced in sympathy and averted his gaze. He knew from experience how mortifying it was when a toddler had a tantrum in public.

"What a racket," Luke muttered, rolling his eyes. "I don't know why people bother bringing little kids to cafés."

The little girl was still crying loudly. Theo overheard the father say, "This isn't going to work. Let me take her to see the fountain while you finish your coffee."

"Okay, thanks, babe," the mum said. "I won't be long."

Theo felt sorry for them. Archie had hated high chairs too. Going out to eat hadn't been worth the stress until he was old enough to sit in a normal chair and do some colouring, or play on Theo's phone while they waited for their food. "Toddlers are pretty unpredictable." Theo said, sharply. "They're dealing with it."

"Oh, yeah. I suppose they are. Sorry I f—" Luke coughed. "I, uh... didn't mean to be a miserable bastard about it. Parents need lives too, I guess."

Theo managed a tight smile. "Yeah. They do." Trying to hide his residual anger, he took a few more gulps of his coffee.

Luke flushed and swirled the coffee around in his now half-empty cup. "I'm sorry. I'm crap at this dating thing aren't I? No wonder I'm still single. Bitching about Christmas music, grumbling about small children. I'll be having a pop at kittens next, or maybe puppies."

Theo chucked, relaxing again as the mood shifted. It did worry him that Luke didn't seem terribly keen on kids. But he was funny, and attractive, and it wasn't as if Archie lived with Theo full-time. If this first date turned into more, Theo could keep the pieces of his life separate for now. "What's wrong with puppies and kittens?"

"Yeah. You got me. I can't find fault with them. They're adorable." Luke lowered his voice. "I actually follow

Tumblrs that post pictures of baby animals. But don't tell anyone, or you'll ruin the miserable bastard reputation I've worked so hard to cultivate."

"Your secret is safe with me."

Luke drained his cup. "So... it feels like a double caffeine kind of evening. And I owe you one. So, if I haven't completely put you off already, what can I get you?"

"I could manage another coffee," Theo wasn't ready for the date to be over yet. "Vanilla latte for me, please. But I need something to eat too."

"What do you fancy?"

"A blueberry muffin please."

Theo watched as Luke walked over to join the queue. It was busy, so he was probably going to be a while. It gave Theo a chance to study him. He was solidly built, with big shoulders, and a nice arse. Theo remembered Luke's hairy chest from his profile pic on Grindr, and he hoped he might eventually get a chance to see it in the flesh along with the rest of him. Theo was smooth, much to his disappointment, and he found body hair on other guys very attractive.

When his perusal of Luke started to border on the creepy, he tore his gaze away and got out his phone instead. He'd put it on silent before coming to meet Luke and found two text messages from Paul on his screen.

Paul: How's the date going? Is he hot?

Paul: Hope he's not an axe murderer. Check in when you can.

Chuckling, Theo typed: *Not an axe murderer, and yeah, he's hot. I think it's going okay. We're having a second cup of coffee.*

Paul replied immediately with: *Always a good sign. Have fun, but use a condom.*

SEVEN

As Luke made his way carefully through the other tables, he saw that Theo had his phone out.

"Here we go," Luke said, putting the tray down on the edge of the table.

Theo put his phone away quickly and moved their old cups out of the way. "Thanks," he said as Luke slid a fresh cup of coffee in his direction. "Can I give you some money for the muffin?" He pulled out his wallet, but Luke waved it away.

"No, no. This is on me. You can get cake on our second date—if we have one."

Theo grinned. "I think we have to have a second date if I owe you cake. I'm pretty sure there's some dating law of the universe to that effect."

"All part of my cunning plan." Luke sat down and passed Theo his muffin. He'd bought carrot cake for himself. "Seriously, though. I'd like to see you again, if you're up for it." He tried to sound casual. It probably wasn't a great idea to have this conversation so soon. It was usually better at the end of the date, or even by text afterwards to avoid face-to-face awkwardness. But he'd brought it up now so decided to roll with it.

"Yeah, I think so. You're not an axe murderer and you bought me cake, so I'd say the chances are good."

"Not an axe murderer? Your standards are low, dude. Anyway how can you be sure? Maybe I left my axe at home."

"Good point. Well, I'll take my chances." Theo broke off a piece of his muffin and put it in his mouth.

The music changed as he chewed, and the familiar opening of "Sleigh Ride" rang out through the speakers.

Luke smirked. "Listen, it's your favourite."

Theo nodded. "Yep," he managed as he finished his mouthful. "It makes me smile."

"Sap," Luke said, forking up a piece of carrot cake.

As they paused the conversation to eat, Luke found himself listening to the song properly for the first time. It was quite fun. When he glanced up he found Theo grinning at him in obvious amusement.

"What?" Luke asked.

"You're bobbing your head in time to the music."

"I was not." Luke promptly stopped tapping his foot under the table.

"You totally were. Admit it. You can't listen to this and not enjoy it." Theo fixed him with a stern look, his soft lips forced into a serious line that was weirdly hot.

Luke sighed. "Yeah, okay. You got me. I will concede that this isn't the worst Christmas song in the world. That title goes to 'Mistletoe and Wine.'"

"Oh yes." Theo laughed. "Now that, we *can* agree on."

They smiled at each other, and as their gazes locked Luke's heart did a little flip. Theo's cheeks flushed and he was the first to look away, but his smile lingered, tugging at the corner of his lips as he sipped his coffee.

I think he's into me. Luke picked up his drink too, hiding his hopeful grin behind the cup.

The rest of the date passed by in a similar vein, with banter and teasing and more discussion of Christmas-related things. They got onto movies next, and then Luke steered it onto gift buying. He was hoping that Theo might mention Archie now they'd talked for a while and got to know each other a little better.

"I always find it a challenge buying gifts for adults," Luke said. "But my family have a fifteen-quid limit on presents for the grown-ups, which helps a bit. My niece and nephew are easy though, there are always loads of things they'd love, and my sister gives me some suggestions. Do you have many people to buy for?"

Theo shrugged. "Not too many I suppose. I don't have a big family, and then there's just a few friends."

"Do you have any brothers and sisters?" Luke asked.

"No."

Luke felt a flash of irritation. Why was Theo being so evasive? Now he wished he'd told Theo that he'd met him while disguised as his Santa alter ego. If he'd done it by message the evening that it happened, everything would be out in the open. As it was, Luke had ended up lying about his job so Theo could tell Luke about Archie in his own time. Now they were both keeping secrets from each other and the whole thing was awkward.

Theo broke the silence that was becoming uncomfortable again. "Tell me more about your sister. What's her name? Do you get on well with her?"

"She's called Lauren, and yeah, we get on great these days." Luke pushed his annoyance aside. "She's two years older than me and we fought all the time when we were growing up. But by the time I turned eighteen we stopped hating each other. She was really supportive when I came out, so that brought us closer together."

"Is she married?"

"Yeah she is. Her husband is called Matthew. He's a good bloke. I see a lot of them and the kids."

A jolt of disappointment twisted Luke's stomach as he remembered that he wouldn't be spending Christmas with them this year. They alternated, staying here for Luke's family one year, and going to Ireland to visit Lauren's in-laws the next. This year was an Ireland year, which meant Luke was going to spend Christmas alone. He could go to his mum's. She lived locally, and he'd be welcome there—in theory. But he always clashed with his stepdad, and without Lauren, Matthew, and the kids to act as buffers it would be way too intense with just the three of them. Luke couldn't face the aggro. He'd told his mum he was staying home to hang out with Charlie so she wouldn't worry about him, but actually Charlie was away with her boyfriend.

Whatever. Christmas was only another day. When he thought about it, all the fuss was ridiculous anyway. Luke wasn't religious, and Christmas was supposed to be all about Jesus and stuff. So what did it matter if he was home alone in sweatpants eating frozen pizza instead of at his mum's eating turkey?

"Luke?" Theo's voice snapped Luke out of his internal pep talk.

"Sorry, I zoned out there for a moment, what did you say?"

"I was asking what your niece and nephew are called?"

"Oh, my nephew is Connor—he's four. And Millie is two." Theo's gaze was intense and Luke felt as if he was being scrutinised. "They're awesome. I love spending time with them."

Theo quirked an eyebrow. "But you don't want any of your own."

Oh, Luke remembered the message conversation where he'd mentioned them to Theo. Was that why he was being so cagey about his situation? Luke couldn't remember exactly what he'd said, but he must have been a bit negative. It was obviously time to attempt some damage limitation.

"Well, I wouldn't rule it out one day," he said cautiously. "It's just that kids are a big responsibility."

"Of course," Theo said.

"Do you want kids?" Luke blurted out, realising it was a mistake as soon as he'd asked the question. *Fuck it.* But he wanted Theo to be honest with him.

Theo's cheeks turned pink and his gaze slid away from Luke's as he gave an uncomfortable huff of laughter. "That's a bit of a serious question for a first date don't you think? Maybe we should see if there's chemistry before we start planning a family."

"Yeah, sorry." Luke forced a chuckle, going along with it, because what else could he do? If they carried on seeing each other, Theo would tell him when he was ready.

Theo looked at his watch. "I'd probably better make a move. I need to get home and eat some food that isn't cake."

"Yeah, me too," Luke replied, relieved at the subject change.

They stood to put on their coats.

"Which way are you walking?" Luke asked. "I'm heading out to the bus station."

"My car is parked out that way. I would offer you a lift but we go in different directions."

"No worries. Can I walk you to your car?" Luke was

hoping for a more intimate goodbye than the brightness and crowds of the shopping centre would allow. He lowered his voice as he fell into step beside Theo. "Then maybe we can test to see if there's chemistry with a kiss goodbye?"

Theo glanced sideways, and gave a shy smile. "I like that plan."

Luke's palm itched with the urge to take Theo's hand, but he didn't know how Theo would feel about such a public display of affection. He settled for walking close beside him until they got through the bright lights and colourful displays of a department store and out into the peace and relative darkness of the car park.

Then Luke did take Theo's hand. "Is this okay?" he asked.

"Yes. Definitely." Theo squeezed for emphasis, and then tugged gently. "My car's this way."

It was freezing outside, their breath hanging in the icy air, but Theo's hand was warm in Luke's and the slow build of excitement and anticipation stopped Luke from feeling the cold.

Theo led Luke past the packed rows of cars, until he finally stopped. "This is mine." Luke didn't drive, and knew fuck-all about cars, but Theo's was small and sensible-looking.

Hand still in Luke's, Theo turned to face him. "Thanks, it was really good to meet you in person."

"You too." Luke's heart rate picked up. He was nervous about making a move, even though there had already been a suggestion of a kiss, but he desperately wanted to.

"And thanks again for the muffin. If we meet up again then it's my turn to buy cake next time." Theo was babbling now, clearly as nervous as Luke was. "I mean, no pressure. If you don't want to see me again, that's fine but—"

"Theo." Luke squeezed his fingers and tugged him closer. Leaning in so their faces were close, Theo's breath warm on his lips, Luke asked, "Is this okay?"

"Yes," Theo said. And then he closed the gap and pressed his lips against Luke's.

Luke let Theo lead. It was a sweet tentative kiss, just a brush of lips. When Theo drew back and licked his lips, Luke wanted more. He let go of Theo's hand and held his shoulders instead. Holding his gaze, he moved in again, closing his eyes as he made contact. Luke started gently, pressing small kisses on Theo's mouth, but then Theo parted his lips with a gasp. He brought his hands up to Luke's hips and pulled him closer, pressing their bodies together as they deepened the kiss. Theo's mouth was addictive, his plush lips as gorgeous as Luke had imagined from his photo. Arousal spread through Luke like the warmth of a log fire, making his body tingle as his dick got hard. With winter layers on, he couldn't tell if Theo was similarly affected at first. But then as Luke slid his tongue against Theo's, Theo moaned in a way that made it pretty obvious the chemistry was mutual.

The clunk of the central locking from a car two away from Theo's made them spring apart, grinning breathlessly at each other. A middle-aged couple were approaching, laden with bags of shopping. If they'd noticed Luke and Theo getting hot and heavy in the car park, they didn't react.

"I should go," Theo said.

"Yeah. And I should hurry and catch my bus. If I miss the next one I'll have to wait another half hour." Luke didn't want to end things there, but it was only a first date and he wasn't sure how Theo would react if Luke asked him back for sex.

"So, uh. Do you want to see me again? You never said." There was a vulnerability to Theo's expression.

"You mean the kiss didn't make it clear?" Luke raised his eyebrows.

"I like to be sure about these things."

"Yes, Theo. I definitely want to see you again. I'll message you later and we can work out when and where."

Theo beamed. "Okay."

Luke gave him a final kiss, just a quick peck on the lips this time. "See you soon."

EIGHT

It was Saturday morning, and Theo was singing along to Christmas music blaring from the car radio on his way to collect Archie.

He'd been on cloud nine ever since his date with Luke. It had been awesome for a first date. The conversation had flowed, and there had definitely been chemistry on both sides. Aside from the slight awkwardness about the kid crying at the next table, and the part where Theo had been evasive about Archie, it had been perfect.

He wondered whether he should have been honest with Luke. But it had only been a first date. He didn't have to tell Luke everything about himself immediately. It wasn't as if he'd actually lied, although he had omitted a rather important detail about his life. He'd considered saying something in a message, but had then decided to wait and see how things went before explaining his situation to Luke. Maybe after a couple more dates—if they had a couple more dates.

Since then, things had been getting increasingly flirty between them via messaging. Luke admitted that he'd considered asking Theo back to his place after their first date, and Theo admitted that he probably would have said yes. They'd arranged a second date for next week—on the Wednesday again—and this time they were going to go out for drinks in the city. Theo felt a thrill of anticipation at the thought of it. After the kiss they'd shared last time, he couldn't imagine that the second date wouldn't go well.

He was still humming to himself as he waited for Caroline to answer the door.

"Hi." She greeted him with a hug. "You look cheerful. Come in for a minute. Archie's busy with his dinosaurs in the living room. It might take a little while to tear him away."

Theo found Archie standing at the coffee table with a load of plastic dinosaurs laid out on the table. They were lined up in a way that looked purposeful, all facing the same direction. Archie held one up and made a roaring sound.

"Hey, Arch. How are you?" Theo knelt beside his son. "Can I have a hug?"

Archie wrapped his arms around Theo's neck, poking him in the ear with his dinosaur while Theo kissed him on the cheek. "Hello, Daddy," he said. "My dinosaurs are going to the zoo."

"Are they?" Theo disengaged himself.

"Yes." Archie put the one he was holding down at the back of one of the lines.

"That's cool. But it's time for you and me to get going, so you might need to tidy these guys up in a minute."

"But I haven't finished!" Archie's tone suggested that it might be better not to rush him.

"Okay, buddy. How about five more minutes then?" Theo was an experienced negotiator by now. "If that's okay with Mummy?" He glanced at Caroline, who nodded.

"Okay." Archie got another dinosaur out of the box on

the floor.

Once the five minutes were up, Archie happily tidied the dinosaurs away—with a little help from Theo—apart from one, which he decided was coming with them, like last week.

"Can we go on the train again?" Archie asked. "I'll bring velociraptor." He pronounced it *veloss-raptor*, but Theo knew what he meant.

"I'm not sure. I thought we might go to the park today." It was sunny outside, which made a nice change after a grey week.

Archie's face fell. "But veloss-raptor likes the train."

"Which train?" Caroline asked.

"The one at the shopping mall," Theo explained. "He loves it." Then to Archie he said, "How about we do both? Park in the morning, and then if you're good I'll take you on the train in the afternoon."

"Yes." Archie grinned. "Train... please," he added as an afterthought.

AFTER A LOVELY COUPLE of hours at the park, Theo was hoping Archie might be tired enough that he could divert him with a DVD instead of battling through the busy shopping mall on a Saturday in December. It was less than two weeks till Christmas now and getting progressively busier. Theo was particularly averse to it, given that he worked there.

However, it was clear that Archie wasn't going to let him get away with staying at home.

"Train, Daddy?" he said as soon as he'd finished his lunch.

Theo sighed. "Yeah, okay then. Go to the toilet and get

your coat and shoes on, then we'll go."

He cleared up the lunch things and went to the toilet himself, and came out to find Archie ready and waiting to leave. He was obviously much more motivated by the promise of a train ride than he was by nursery in the morning when he took forever to get his shoes on.

"Ready." Archie was standing by the front door with his velociraptor in one hand, and the small cuddly toy that he'd got from Santa last weekend in the other. It was a purple elephant—christened Mr Purple by Archie—and Archie had slept with it in his bed all week. "Mr Purple wants to come too."

As expected, the shopping mall was hectic. It took Theo a while to find a parking space, but he managed to get a parent and child one eventually. As they walked to the entrance, they had to pass Santa's Grotto.

Archie stopped, tugging on Theo's hand. "Can I see Santa again?"

"Not today, Archie. We're going on the train, remember?"

"But I want to say thank you for Mr Purple," Archie said earnestly. "He's my fave-rit."

Mr Purple was currently clutched in Archie's spare hand, while Theo had been given the job of carrying the velociraptor.

Theo chuckled. It was hard to say no to Archie when he was being adorable, and it didn't cost that much to visit Santa. Five quid was decent value for the cuddly toy and a bit of time in the grotto doing some colouring when you compared it to a cup of fancy coffee and a hot chocolate for Archie. "Okay. Let's get a ticket now, and then we can come back after going on the train."

THE TIMING WORKED OUT PERFECTLY. After they'd queued for the train and had their ride, it was time for them to go back to Santa's Grotto for their slot. Archie was starting to flag now but he was still excited at the prospect of seeing Santa again. Apparently he'd made quite an impression last week.

Archie played alongside some other kids in the grotto while they waited. When the elf finally called their number, Theo went to get him.

"Time to see Santa again."

Archie's face lit up. With Mr Purple in one hand and his velociraptor in the other, he marched happily ahead of Theo towards the archway, nothing like the shy little boy of last week. Theo had to hurry to keep up.

"Hello, young man," Santa boomed in his obviously fake jolly voice. "What's your name?"

"I'm Archie, and this is my daddy, Theo," Archie enunciated clearly.

Santa jerked his head up and blue eyes met Theo's for a moment. Theo gave a small slightly embarrassed smile and a wave.

"Oh yes of course," Santa said in a loud, cheerful voice. "I remember you from last week, Archie, and your dad. What an unexpected pleasure to see you both again."

Archie climbed into Santa's lap without waiting to be asked this week. "You gave me Mr Purple. He's my fave-rit." He held up the elephant for Santa's inspection. "Thank you."

"You're very welcome." Amusement softened Santa's tone. "So, Archie. Have you been a good boy since I saw you last?"

"Yes," Archie said seriously, then in a typical four-year-old segue he added. "I went on the train again."

"Oh, good. Good." Santa glanced at Theo, and it was hard to tell, but Theo thought he was smiling under the huge white beard that hid most of his face. "And who's this you've brought to see me as well as Mr Purple?"

"He's a veloss-raptor."

"Does he have a name?"

"No." Archie frowned. "Dinosaurs don't have names. Only cuddly things."

"I see. So, Archie. Are you excited about Christmas?"

"Yes. I'm going to Mummy's house and I'll get presents, and Mummy said I can have chocolate for breakfast."

Theo snorted. "I'm pretty sure she didn't, Arch. But you might get a little bit of chocolate in your stocking."

"So what's your daddy doing at Christmas, if he doesn't have you to keep him busy? Does he get a lie-in?"

Santa's tone was jovial, but Theo bristled at the line of questioning. It touched a raw nerve, and really it was none of Santa's bloody business what Theo's Christmas plans were. He met Santa's gaze and those blue eyes were scrutinising him, Theo felt as if they were looking for weakness.

"Just a quiet Christmas alone for me," Theo said briskly. "I get to chill out and recharge my batteries before Archie comes to me for Boxing Day—which is our honorary Christmas celebration, so Archie gets two Christmases."

"Wow. Do you get to have turkey twice?" Santa asked Archie. "Lucky you."

"No. Daddy said we can have cheese on toast. Didn't you, Daddy?" Archie turned to Theo for confirmation.

"Sure did, buddy. I'm quite happy not to have to cook a Christmas dinner." Theo wasn't much of a cook, and the organisation required for a roast was definitely beyond him.

"Well, that sounds like fun," Santa said. "I hope you both have a good time. Now, Archie, let me see what I have for you today." He reached down into the sack of presents and sifted through them, selecting a gift wrapped in red paper with yellow stars on. Holding it out to Archie, he said, "Here you go."

"Thank you." Archie remembered his manners this week. "Daddy hold these." He held out Mr Purple and the dinosaur for Theo to take. "Can I open it now?"

Santa looked at Theo. "Is that okay with your dad?"

"Sure." Theo shrugged. "As long as we're not holding up your queue."

"No. It won't take long."

Sure enough, Archie ripped the paper off in a flash.

"Ooh. It's a pig, and it's blue. Look, Daddy."

It was another cuddly toy; Theo suspected that all the presents in Santa's sack were along those lines. "Oh, he's nice. What are you going to call him?"

"I think it's a girl pig. So she's Mrs Blue," Archie announced. "She can sleep in my bed too."

"Okay then, Archie, we'd better say goodbye to Santa now, because I'm sure he has lots of other children to see." Theo glanced at Santa and smiled. It was hard to tell if Santa was smiling back. "Thank you."

"You're very welcome," Santa said as Archie slid off his lap, Mrs Blue in his hand.

"I want Mr Purple," Archie held his hand out for the elephant. "You keep the veloss-raptor. Don't lose him."

"Such a responsibility," Santa said with a wink to Theo.

"I know, right? They don't warn you about this in the parenting books." Theo grinned.

"Bye bye, Santa," Archie said. "Come on, Daddy."

"Goodbye, Archie," Santa said.

Theo raised a hand in farewell. "Thanks."

NINE

Luke had arranged to meet Theo for a drink at a gay-friendly pub in the city. It was a bus ride away from home for both of them, but it would allow them to drink—and hopefully flirt—without worrying about attracting any unwanted attention out in the suburbs where they lived.

Excited about seeing Theo again, Luke ended up getting an earlier bus than he needed, so he killed some time wandering around the city centre shops for a while. Bundled up in thick coats against the chill, a choir were singing carols with great gusto. Luke stopped to listen for a while, and then put a couple of quid in their charity collection bucket.

A little further along, he paused in front of an elaborate window display in a department store. Leafless metal trees strung with Christmas lights stood in a landscape of fake snow and glitter against a backdrop of an alpine-looking scene, while shop dummies modelled the latest winter fashions. Outside, the weather echoed the display as tiny flakes of sleet started to drift from the dark sky. Luke shivered, ready to get into the warmth of the pub. It was proper winter weather today.

His phone buzzed in his pocket, and he pulled it out to see a message from Theo.

Theo: I'm on my way.

Luke replied, asking: *What time does your bus get in?*

Theo: Should be about 7:50 if it's on time.

That was in about twenty minutes.

Luke: I'll meet you at the bus station.

Theo: Okay :)

Pacing back and forth at the bus station, Luke was all keyed up with nerves and excitement as he waited. It felt like ages since their date last week, and he was impatient to spend time with Theo again—without the disguise of his Santa suit. Luke couldn't believe it when Theo and Archie had turned up for the second week in a row. Seeing Theo had reminded Luke how cute he was, and watching him with Archie only made Luke like him even more. He was so sweet with his kid, patient, and good-humoured. Luke reckoned that said a lot about a person.

When the subject of Christmas plans had come up, Luke hadn't been able to resist digging to see what Theo was doing. Now he knew that Theo was supposed to be spending Christmas alone, Luke was hopeful that maybe he could persuade Theo to do something with him instead, as long as this second date went well. Luke was nervous about asking though, somehow asking a guy he'd only kissed once to spend Christmas with him seemed like kind of a big deal. But if neither of them had plans, then why not? All he could do was ask.

As Theo's bus pulled into its bay, Luke's heart beat faster in anticipation. Then there he was, dressed in jeans and a black woollen coat, absorbed in wrapping a bright red scarf around his neck as he stepped off the bus in a flow of people. Luke was already smiling when Theo finally looked up and saw him, and Theo's answering smile made Luke's heart sing like the Christmas carollers he'd heard in the city centre earlier.

"Hey," Luke said as Theo approached.

"Hi." Theo's smile widened.

Luke held his arms open and Theo walked into the hug he offered. Luke wanted to kiss him, but surrounded by people he wasn't sure if Theo would want that. So he settled for a hug that was definitely a little longer, and involved more body contact, than just a friendly hug would, but wasn't enough to draw attention.

When they separated, Theo's cheeks were flushed. "It's really good to see you again."

"You too." They grinned at each other for a moment, foolish and smitten—well Luke was, and Theo was certainly giving those signals as well. "Pub?" Luke finally said.

"Yeah, definitely. Let's go."

They walked back the way Luke had come to meet him, past the older more rundown parts of the city centre first where the sleet was still falling, and then on through a newer covered section that was lit up with strings of lights and elaborate decorations. A huge white Christmas tree that looked to be made entirely of lights dominated the central space.

"Wow." Theo paused to look at it. "I've only been past this in the daytime. It's amazing in the dark."

"Yeah, stunning," Luke agreed. But he was looking at Theo's upturned face and smile of wonder rather than at the tree.

The pub was tucked away behind the new shopping centre, not obvious unless you knew where it was. Luke had been there a few times with friends, so he knew it was queer-friendly although it wasn't in the gay district of the city. The owners sometimes hosted fundraisers for the LGBT community, and they had gender neutral toilets. It seemed like a safe place to bring Theo on a date.

They entered through a paved courtyard outdoors where a couple of people sat smoking, through a room with clusters of tables around an open space that was sometimes used as a dance floor, and into the main bar at the back. This early in the evening, the pub was quiet with plenty of tables free. It was the sort of place that didn't really fill up until much later. In some ways it was more like a club in that regard, although the dark wood panelling and tatty decor was all pub.

"What do you want to drink?" Luke asked.

"A pint of whatever beer looks nice," Theo said, scanning the labels on the pumps. "I'll try the IPA."

"Two pints of IPA please," Luke said to the barman. Luke was usually more of a lager man, but ale seemed suitable in this cosy pub now they were out of the cold.

Once they had their drinks, they went to sit at a small corner table and filled the momentary awkward silence by taking sips of their beer.

"That's nice," Theo said.

"Yeah?" Luke wasn't really an ale connoisseur. As long as it didn't taste of vinegar he couldn't tell much difference.

"Yes, it's not too hoppy, and has got a hint of sweetness. I like that."

"You know your beer then?" Luke took another sip. He could see what Theo meant now he'd pointed it out.

"Yes. My dad's a real ale fan. He does a bit of home brewing too."

Theo hadn't mentioned his family much, so Luke asked,

"What are your parents like? You haven't said a lot about them, other than that they live up north. But you can't be from there because you don't have the accent."

"They relocated when I was at uni because of Dad's job. Before that we lived near Reading."

"Do you see much of them?"

"I try and get up there at least a couple of times a year and they come down to visit too. We're pretty close. Being an only child meant they were very focused on me when I was growing up, but in a good way."

"They're okay about you being gay?"

"Absolutely." Theo nodded fervently. "I told them when I was about fourteen. My mum was the first person I told. I was scared about telling friends, but I knew she'd be on my side."

"That's good." Luke felt a pang of envy. His coming out at home hadn't gone so smoothly, but that was mainly due to his dad rather than his mum. His mum had only been unsupportive because she was frightened of how his dad would react—with good reason as it turned out. His dad hadn't taken it well, and it had caused a lot of family strife. Luke still blamed himself for his parents' divorce, even though his mum assured him that the problems were there long before she'd had to side with Luke against his father. He had no contact with his dad now, and had been very close to his mum until she remarried. Now things were tense again. Not because his stepdad was homophobic per se, but because he was quite right wing in his politics in general, and Luke always ended up arguing with him about something.

"Yeah. I'm lucky it was so easy. How was it with your family?"

"Eh, it was tricky at first," Luke said. "But it's okay now.

My mum and sister are cool, and I don't see my dad since my parents split up." He didn't want to spoil the mood by talking about his dad, so he changed the subject quickly. "Where did you go to uni?"

They chatted about their education for a while. Theo had a degree in maths, so Luke teased him for being a geek. Luke had studied history, which he'd enjoyed, but hadn't really helped him with graduate jobs unless he'd wanted to go into teaching—which he didn't. They grumbled about the state of the job market and how difficult it was for their generation.

Over their second pint they got onto hobbies. Theo was more into reading than Luke—mainly sci-fi and literary fiction, where Luke was more of a film buff. They both liked gaming, although Theo preferred strategy games, and Luke liked letting off steam with faster paced action games.

When their second drinks were empty, Luke stood up. "It's my round. Do you want another?"

"Maybe just a half," Theo said. "I'm not a big drinker."

"Me neither. Not these days anyway." Luke used to overdo it on a regular basis when he was a student, but not anymore. Alcohol was an expensive habit and only made it harder to get up for work.

He got halves for both of them, and when he got back to the table he sat on the bench seat beside Theo instead of opposite. They were close together, knees touching, and Luke put a hand on Theo's leg under the table. "Is this okay?"

"Yes." Theo shuffled closer so their thighs were pressed together. Luke left his hand where it was. The contact was nice, and Theo seemed happy with it.

"Do you think they're on a date too?" Luke nodded in the direction of a couple who were seated a few tables over.

They were both gender ambiguous and it was hard to judge whether they were male or female, or neither. Luke didn't suppose it mattered. They looked happy and as if they were enjoying each other's company.

As they watched, the couple held hands over the table, lacing their fingers together, and smiling in a way that was more than friendly.

"Yeah. I reckon so." Theo put his hand on top of Luke's, stroking Luke's fingers lightly. His touch sent a shiver of anticipation through Luke and he squeezed Theo's thigh reflexively.

Luke turned to look at Theo, who gave a shy smile. "Can I kiss you?"

Theo nodded, and that was all the encouragement Luke needed. Putting his drink down, he cupped Theo's cheek with the hand that wasn't on his leg, and guided him into a kiss. He kept it quick, they were in public after all, but it wasn't entirely chaste.

When Luke drew back, Theo's pupils were blown wide.

"I wish we were alone so we could do more of that," Luke said.

"Me too." Theo's voice was husky and he kept his gaze on Luke as though he couldn't look away.

"Come back to my place? You can stay over if you want?" Luke blurted. They hadn't planned further than a drink in town for this date, but his inhibitions were lowered by arousal and alcohol. He wanted Theo in his bed.

Theo seemed to consider it for a moment, and then his face broke into a mischievous grin as though they were about to do something forbidden. "Okay."

Luke hadn't expected him to agree so easily. He blinked. "Really?"

"Yes." A shrug of Theo's shoulders, then an amused

glint in his eye as he added, "Unless you've changed your mind already."

"No. Definitely not." Luke looked at his watch. "There's a bus in about fifteen minutes. We can probably make that one if we hurry."

"Okay." Theo picked up his glass and drank.

Luke did the same, draining his half pint before Theo could change his mind.

TEN

Theo was squeezed in next to the bus window, his breath fogging the glass as the bus gradually carried them away from the city centre and out to the suburbs. With Luke's hand warm on his thigh, Theo's cock was half hard, a pleasant throb of anticipation that built when Luke started to move his fingers in tiny circles.

Theo shifted, adjusting himself discreetly. But Luke caught the movement and gave him a wicked grin. He leaned in and whispered, "I'm hard too." His breath was warm and ticklish by Theo's ear. It didn't help Theo's situation at all.

It felt as if the bus halted at every single bus stop along the way. Theo resisted groaning out loud every time another passenger rang the bell. Caught up in impatience to be alone with Luke, he didn't question whether he was doing the right thing. He wanted Luke badly and was following his instincts rather than reason. It wasn't till they got off the bus and the shock of the freezing night air cut through Theo's haze of tipsy lust that he wondered if he was making a mistake. Should he really be considering sleeping with

Luke when he was keeping secrets from him? Maybe he should tell Luke about Archie before he let things get more serious between them.

But as the bus pulled away, Luke took Theo's hand and led him into a pool of darkness between two street lamps and pushed him up against a brick wall. His mouth was hot and insistent, and the kiss stripped away any last reservations Theo had. He wanted Luke, he needed this, was desperate for more of it... more of Luke. It was only a second date, and it was only sex, not a promise of anything more. Luke didn't need to know everything about Theo's life any more than Theo needed to know about his. Until they knew for sure they had chemistry there was no point making things any more complicated than this. His desire for Luke was real and raw, and entirely honest. That was all that mattered for now.

He put his arms around Luke's neck, deepening the kiss as Luke slid his hands inside Theo's open coat to grip his hips. They ground together, hard and eager until Theo moaned.

Luke pulled away, breathless and chuckling. "Sorry. I got carried away."

"How far is it to yours?" Theo asked. "Because we might be alone here at the moment, but I'd rather not get arrested for indecent exposure."

"It's not far, just a few minutes." Luke took his hand. "Come on."

Luke led him along a street of terraced houses, before stopping at one and getting his keys out of his pocket. "This is my place. I'm in the upstairs flat."

Theo followed Luke indoors and up a flight of steps to another door. Latin music boomed on the other side as Luke unlocked it.

"I take it you don't live alone then?" Theo realised how little they knew about each other. He hadn't given any thought to Luke's living arrangements. Of course, many people their age lived in flat shares; it was expensive to live alone—as Theo knew all too well. But he didn't want anyone else around when he was in dad-mode, so he managed by cutting back on other costs where he could.

"Oh, no. Sorry, I should have said. I have a flatmate, Charlie." He opened the door into a small hallway, where the music assaulted Theo's ears. "Come in. I'll introduce you."

He led Theo through a door on the left into a small kitchen.

Expecting a guy, Theo was surprised to find that Charlie was female. Oblivious to their presence, she was washing up with her back to the kitchen doorway, wiggling her arse in time to the music and singing along to "La Bamba."

"Hey, honey, I'm home," Luke said loudly over the music.

Charlie jumped and turned around with a rubber-gloved hand to her chest. "Fucking hell, Luke. You scared the crap out of me. I wasn't expecting you back this early!" Then her gaze lit on Theo and her expression changed to one of amusement. "Oh. So the date is going well then?"

"Yes, it is thank you." Luke seemed totally unfazed. "Charlie, Theo. Theo, Charlie."

Theo raised his hand, cheeks flushing warm. "Hi."

"Nice to meet you." Charlie waggled her yellow-clad fingers in return.

"So, we're just gonna...." Luke jerked his head vaguely towards the kitchen door and Theo's cheeks burned hotter.

"Okay. Have fun. I'll keep the music nice and loud." She turned back to her washing up.

Luke led Theo back into the hallway where he toed out of his shoes and hung up his coat, so Theo followed suit.

"This is my room, and that's the bathroom next to it if you need." Luke gestured to a door that stood ajar before opening the door into his room and turning a light on.

"No. I'm good." Theo followed Luke into his room. He didn't have time to take much in, other than a vague awareness of a fairly tidy looking room and a double bed with a light blue duvet cover, because as soon as he shut the door Luke moved in to kiss him. Like a switch being flipped, all the sexual tension between them was back, and there was nothing to stop them following through with it now.

They kissed each other hungrily, letting their hands search under clothes for skin to stroke. Theo shivered as Luke sucked on his neck. His beard scratched deliciously and Theo put his head to one side to give him better access as he fumbled with the fly on Luke's jeans. Luke worked on Theo's shirt buttons, managing to undo a few before Theo got his hand in Luke's pants to stroke his cock, and then Luke seemed to forget about undressing Theo; too busy moaning and thrusting into his grip as their mouths locked again, wet and desperate.

Finally, Luke broke away panting. "Stop that, or I'm going to come." He looked wrecked already, cheeks flushed, his hard cock sticking out of his jeans and shining wet at the tip.

Theo wanted it in his mouth, but that wouldn't help Luke last. "How about we get some clothes off while you have a breather?" he suggested.

"Yeah. I like that plan."

They undressed quickly, and Luke turned on a lamp by

the bed. "Can you turn the main light off?" He asked Theo who was closer.

"Sure." As Theo crossed back to the bed, Luke was already lying down, naked and hard. Theo crawled over and straddled him, their cocks bumping as they kissed again. When Theo reckoned Luke had calmed down a little, he started to work his way down Luke's body. He kissed his neck and then nuzzled the hair on his chest, finding a nipple and kissing that too. Luke stiffened and gasped, so Theo did it again, looking up to see Luke's reaction as he used his tongue on the hard nub.

"Fuck," Luke muttered.

"That good?" Theo asked.

"Yeah. My nipples are ridiculously sensitive."

"Good to know." Theo grinned, moving across to lick and suck the other one and making Luke squirm and groan before he moved lower still. Luke's body was hot. Not gym toned, but strong and solid, and the hair on his torso was gorgeous. It thickened into a dark trail in the centre of his belly, and Theo followed it down, bypassing Luke's cock to kiss his balls instead.

"Tease," Luke grumbled.

"I thought you didn't want to come too fast." Theo pushed Luke's legs apart and Luke moved with him, tilting his hips up.

"Yeah. Maybe I changed my mind." Luke reached for his cock and stroked it a few times while Theo watched. But when a bead of precome appeared at the tip, he pushed Luke's hand away and wrapped his fingers around in their place.

"I want to taste you. Can I?"

"Fuck yes." He thrust up into Theo's grip.

Theo lowered his head and took Luke in his mouth,

swiping into the slit to catch the precome. Then he took him deeper, seeing if he could manage it all. Luke wasn't huge but he had a nice cock, thick and straight, and very hard. It nudged the back of Theo's throat and Luke groaned, bringing his hands down to hold Theo's head. He didn't push or force, but his whole body was taut with tension and need.

Wanting to please him, Theo sucked, bobbing his head and using his tongue to stroke and swirl. Luke started to push up to meet Theo's mouth, his hips lifting eagerly as Theo fondled his balls before reaching back to rub Luke's hole with a fingertip. "Fuck, Theo," he gasped. "You're going to make me come if you carry on."

Theo pulled off long enough to say. "I'm okay with that, if you are?"

"Yeah. Totally."

So Theo started to suck him again. He loved giving head, loved making another guy feel good, and watching Luke fall apart under his mouth and hands had Theo hard and eager too. He ground his hips into the bed, thrusting against the covers as he sucked Luke harder and faster. Finally Luke groaned and tensed, and his cock pulsed against Theo's tongue. Theo hummed his encouragement and swallowed, forcing down the bitter saltiness, and then carried on sucking more gently until Luke's body relaxed, his hands flopping away from Theo's head.

"God that was amazing," Luke said huskily.

"Yeah?" Theo grinned, moving up to lie beside him. He threw an arm over Luke's chest and snuggled close to kiss his cheek.

Luke turned his head and kissed him on the lips. "Yeah." He reached down to palm Theo's erection. "I'll take care of you in a minute."

"No rush," Theo said. And although he was horny as hell, he meant it. This was nice too, lying and exchanging slow, sensual kisses. There was no hurry for more; they had plenty of time—maybe even all night if Theo decided to stay. Luke had offered, and Theo thought he'd wait and see how it went. He didn't have work till twelve tomorrow, so he would have plenty of time to get a bus home in the morning.

After a while, Luke rolled onto his side and deepened the kiss, taking Theo in hand and starting to stroke in a steady rhythm that soon had Theo breathing hard and thrusting into Luke's fist. Luke was getting hard again too; Theo could feel him against his hip.

Breaking the kiss, Luke asked, "What do you want to do?"

"I don't mind," Theo said. "I just want to come." His balls felt full and heavy.

"Do you want me to blow you? Or you could fuck me if you want?"

"Yeah. I'd love to fuck you." Theo hadn't topped in ages. He rarely hooked up anyway, and the last few guys he'd been with they'd either traded blow jobs, or Theo had been the one to get fucked. His skinny, twink looks tended to attract tops when he was out in bars or clubs.

"Let me get some lube and a condom." Luke twisted away to reach in the drawer by the bed, and Theo admired his arse. It was full and muscular and he couldn't wait to fuck it. "How do you want to do this?" Luke asked as he handed Theo a condom and put the lube down on the bed.

"On your front. If that's okay?"

"Yeah. Definitely."

Luke got on all fours in the middle of the bed, and Theo moved behind him, sitting on his heels to roll on the condom. "Fuck, you look hot like that." Luke was gorgeous. Broad shoulders tapering down to that perfect juicy arse.

Condom on, Theo gripped Luke's buttocks and bent down to kiss first one, then the other. He did it again, and then again, working his way closer to Luke's hole each time.

"Theoooo," Luke drew out the sound impatiently.

Chuckling, Theo finally put his mouth where Luke wanted it, breathing in his musky scent and a hint of shower gel, circling his tongue as Luke moaned. "That good?" he asked, using his fingers in place of his tongue for a moment.

"Yeah."

So Theo licked him again, pressing a little harder this time, and feeling the muscle give. He carried on as Luke's sounds got louder and more needy, until finally Luke said, "Fuck, Theo. Give me your cock."

Theo's cock was more than ready to be inside, rock hard and eager as he stroked some lube on himself. Then he put a little on Luke's hole, dipping in with one finger and then two, making sure Luke was ready to take him. "You good to go?" he asked.

"Yeah. Do it."

Lining himself up, Theo pushed carefully inside, just the tip first. It felt so good, a tight hot squeeze around the head of his cock. "Okay?"

"Yes." Luke pressed back. "More." Theo obliged, thrusting in as deep as he could go. They both groaned at the sensation. "Yeah, come on. Fuck me."

Theo gripped Luke's hips and started slowly, fucking him with long steady slides. He was close already, after being on the edge for so long, but this pace would stop him getting there too soon. "Do you think you can come again?" he asked breathlessly. If Luke might be able to go again, he wanted to try to wait for him.

"Yeah. I reckon."

Luke got a hand underneath himself and Theo could see the movement of his elbow as he jerked himself off. Theo fucked him a little faster, biting his lip to distract himself with the sting of it. Luke moaned, breathing hard, his arm working furiously now.

"Yes," Luke gasped. "Harder."

Theo really fucking hoped Luke was nearly there, because he was, and if he went harder it would probably finish him off. He thrust in again, giving Luke everything he had, and was rewarded when Luke groaned. "Fuck, yes. I'm going to come."

The hot squeeze and pulse around Theo's cock as Luke came pulled Theo over the edge with him. He cried out, filling the condom as he thrust in one last time. When he was done he draped himself over Luke's back and kissed his shoulder. His skin was soft, and damp with sweat. "That was awesome," he murmured.

"Yeah," Luke said, still out of breath. "Yeah it was. Fuck, my legs are shaking."

Theo chuckled, taking his weight off him. "I'll take that as a compliment." He withdrew carefully and dealt with the condom, tying it off, and dropping it on the floor by the bed.

"You should." Luke knelt up. "Pass me a tissue." He gestured to the box by the bed.

Theo passed him the whole box, and Luke wiped the come off his duvet, before pulling the covers back and getting into the bed and patting the space beside him. Theo went to fill it, moving easily into Luke's embrace. They traded a lazy sated kiss, and then Theo put his head on Luke's shoulder. It felt easy and comfortable, as though they'd done this many times before.

ELEVEN

Luke knew he had a daft grin on his face, but he couldn't stop himself. Luckily Theo was tucked under Luke's arm, his head on Luke's shoulder, so he couldn't see how goofy Luke looked right now. Good sex did that to a person, Luke told himself, and it always left you happy and buzzing. But he suspected it was more than just the good sex that was making him smile. It was everything about Theo.

The evening had been so good: easy conversation, great kissing, and amazing sex. It really couldn't have gone better. Riding high on the success of it all, Luke decided he wasn't going to find a better time to bring up the subject of Christmas plans.

"So... you said your parents live right up in Northumberland. It's a long way to travel. Do you get enough time off at Christmas to visit?" Luke felt a little bad about his line of questioning. It seemed dishonest when he already knew Theo was going to be home alone for Christmas, but fuck it. He was doing it with good intentions, and it wasn't as if Theo was being entirely honest with him either.

"Yeah, it is a long way. It would be hard to fit it in this

year around work." Theo's disappointment was evident in his tone. Now was Luke's chance.

"So have you got other plans closer to home?" Luke's heart beat faster, and he braced himself ready to make his invitation. Surely Theo would rather hang out with Luke than spend Christmas alone.

There was a slight pause before Theo answered. "Um... yeah. I'm spending it with some friends of mine. Paul and Jolyon. They're a couple so I'll be playing third wheel, but it was nice of them to invite me, and it's definitely better than being a lonely saddo and spending Christmas on my own, right?"

Ouch.

"Oh, yeah. Yeah of course. Nobody wants to be that guy," Luke managed, while internally he cursed. He hadn't anticipated Theo flat out lying to him. The slight hesitation before answering made him suspect that Theo wasn't actually spending Christmas with these alleged friends, and unless his plans had changed since Saturday it seemed unlikely he was being truthful.

"What about you?" Theo asked. "Will you be doing stuff with your family?"

"Uh... yeah. Yeah of course. Hanging out at my mum's and eating my bodyweight in turkey, as you do." The lie tripped off Luke's tongue easily. Theo wasn't the only one who could make stuff up, apparently, and Luke didn't want to be the only one admitting to Billy-No-Mates Christmas plans. "I don't get on great with my stepdad but it's worth going there for my mum's cooking." That part was true at least, maybe Luke should reconsider accepting his mum's invitation if it was still open.

"Yeah. I wish I could go and see my folks, but it's just not feasible this year."

The conversation ground to a halt, and the silence grew heavy between them. Luke's earlier smile had melted away, along with his good mood, and he lay stiff and uncomfortable with Theo's head an awkward weight on his shoulder rather than a welcome one. Deception had thrown up an invisible barrier between them, eroding the intimacy of earlier. Maybe Theo felt it too, because he rolled away saying, "I need to use your toilet."

Luke closed his eyes for a moment, listening to the rustle of clothing as Theo dressed and the sound of his door opening and closing.

When Theo came back, he stood awkwardly at the foot of the bed in his jeans and T-shirt, making no move to rejoin Luke under the covers. "I should probably call a taxi or something. I know you said I could stay over, but I have work in the morning, so it would be easier if I make it home." His expression was hard to read, a hint of worry, and maybe a dash of hope. Did he want Luke to try to persuade him to stay?

"Okay." Earlier Luke would have encouraged him to sleep here even though he had an early start for work too. But now his bubble of happy hopefulness had burst he didn't want Theo in his bed for the night. The secrets between them loomed, seemingly insurmountable. Luke wanted to fix things and make it right, but he didn't know how.

He got out of bed, naked and exposed as he picked up a pair of sweatpants from the back of his chair and quickly pulled them on, followed by a T-shirt. "I've got a couple of taxi numbers on my phone." He retrieved his phone from his jeans where he'd left it earlier. "Here. Just hit call."

Theo tried a couple of numbers before he found one

that could come and get him soon. "Twenty minutes." He handed the phone back to Luke who pocketed it.

"Do you want a quick cup of tea or anything?" Luke asked, wanting to find a focus while they waited. The awkwardness between them was almost palpable and he wondered what Theo made of it, because of course Theo only knew about his own dishonesty. He didn't know about Luke's.

"Um. Yeah, okay. Thanks."

Luke led the way to the kitchen. The sound of the television came from the living room, so Charlie was obviously still up. He put the kettle on and made them both some Redbush tea. Theo had his black, and Luke topped it up with cold water so he'd be able to drink it before his taxi came. "Want to go and sit in the living room?" The TV would remove the need for conversation, and right now that was appealing. Suddenly this felt like just another awkward hook up to Luke. The sooner he could get shot of Theo the better. He needed space to work out whether it was possible to salvage things between them, and to decide whether he even wanted to.

Charlie was lying on the sofa watching *Family Guy*, and she greeted them with a smile and a knowing look as they sat in the two armchairs, but thankfully she didn't try and stop the TV to chat to them.

When the doorbell buzzed, Luke and Theo both got up. "That'll probably be the taxi."

"Bye, Theo," Charlie said.

"Bye."

Luke spoke to the driver via the intercom. "He'll be down in a sec." He turned to Theo in the bright light of the hallway. Theo faced him, he had a pinched expression. "I had a good time tonight, thank you."

"Me too," Luke said, forcing a grin. That wasn't a lie, because until the last half hour it had been wonderful. It wasn't fair to blame Theo for the weirdness now when Luke was partly responsible.

Theo's face smoothed out into an answering smile. "I'd like to see you again. If you want?"

"Sure." Luke *wasn't* sure. But he wasn't going to rush into a decision tonight. "I'll message you later, or tomorrow. You'd better hurry. Taxi drivers hate waiting." He gave Theo a quick kiss on the cheek and a hug, which Theo returned, squeezing him hard.

"Bye, Luke."

LUKE WENT BACK into the living room and flopped down by Charlie's feet with a sigh.

"What's up?" She paused the TV. "You should be all smiley and glowing with a post-sex high, surely? Did something happen?"

"Ugh. It's really complicated, and kind of a long story."

She sat up, facing him. "We've got time. Come on, spill."

So Luke explained the mess of deception he and Theo had got themselves into. Going over it all didn't make it feel any better, and Luke still wasn't sure how to fix it.

"So you know he's lying to you, but he doesn't know you know about it?"

"Yep."

"And you're lying to him too?"

"Yes," Luke said miserably. "It's a mess. I mean... I could just come clean and tell him that I'm Santa, and that I know about Archie, and that he's going to be alone for Christmas like me. But I'm not sure if that would help. Does it seem really creepy that I didn't tell him straight away when I recognised him? I didn't want to out him as a dad before he was ready to tell me himself."

"No. I can see why you kept quiet about it." She frowned. "Why do you think he hasn't told you yet?"

"I don't know." That was still bugging Luke too. "Maybe he thinks I won't want to date a guy with a child? I guess some men might not want that complication. But if the relationship was ever going to go anywhere he'd have had to tell me eventually. Maybe he doesn't really want a relationship. He might be one of those guys who's only on Grindr for sex. I didn't get that vibe from him though."

"Maybe he was waiting for the right time to tell you. This was only your second date."

"I know. The stupid thing is that if I didn't know about Archie at this stage it wouldn't matter. It's only awkward because I *do* know, and he doesn't *know* I know."

Charlie snorted.

"Stop it. It's not funny," Luke grumbled, yet he smiled despite himself. And when Charlie started laughing, he couldn't help chuckling too. "Okay, I guess it is kind of funny because it's a ridiculous situation. But it's not funny when it's happening to *me*. I really like him, Charlie, and I don't want to fuck things up before we've even had a chance to get started. I don't know how to fix it."

"Unless you want to drag it all out in the open, I think you have to wait for him to tell you about Archie when he's ready."

"Yeah. I suppose so. But in the meantime it's really hard acting normal around him."

"I can see that. So maybe leave it a while before you meet again. Keep talking, but have a bit of physical space?"

"Yeah, perhaps that's for the best."

"And you know what?" Charlie said. "If you guys end up together, this whole shitshow will make an awesome anecdote for your best man's speech."

Luke chuckled. "Yeah. That's true."

LATER, Luke's phone buzzed as he was lying in bed thinking about turning his light off.

Theo: Thanks again for a fun and hot evening ;)

Luke smiled, his mood lifting a little more. Maybe Charlie was right, if they got past this ridiculous start to their relationship, it might be something they could laugh about eventually.

Luke: The pleasure was all mine. Well, not quite all. But as I got to cum twice I think I came out on top.

Theo: I'm pretty sure I was on top.

Luke: LOL

Theo: So, I'm free on Friday night if you want to meet again soon?

Luke stared at the screen. He was torn between wanting to see Theo again and worrying that it would be weird and awkward while there were still too many secrets between them. Luke was afraid that face-to-face the temptation to spill everything would be too much. He couldn't handle another conversation like the one they'd had this evening. It would be best to leave things till after Christmas, let the dust settle, and in the meantime he could try and coax some honesty out of Theo while they talked.

Luke: Sorry. I have plans on Friday.

Theo: Oh, okay. Another time then.

Luke was relieved that Theo didn't suggest another date. He'd have felt like an arsehole fobbing him off twice.

Luke: I'm knackered now; somebody wore me out earlier, so I'd better hit the sack.

Theo: Yeah, me too :)

Luke: Night x

Theo: xx

STILL WANTING headspace when he got up the next day, Luke saw that Theo had sent him a "good morning" message, but he didn't open it. Instead he scrolled through Facebook while he ate his breakfast, and then listened to music on the bus when he'd normally chat with Theo. He headed into work feeling despondent. Why was dating so fucking complicated?

He waited until lunchtime to reply to Theo's message.

Luke: Hey, belated good morning to you too. Crazy busy here. Hope your day is going well.

It showed as delivered, but not read. Theo was probably busy at work. That spared Luke the need to try to make conversation for a little while longer. Sitting in Starbucks finishing his coffee, Luke watched the flow of shoppers passing by. He sighed, feeling lonely despite the crowds surrounding him. The decorations everywhere seemed to mock his lack of festive spirit and as his brain keyed into the music that was playing he gave a humourless huff at the irony. Elvis Presley singing about being lonely at Christmas was rubbing salt into the wound.

Checking his watch, Luke realised he needed to hurry up. He had to get back to the grotto and into his Santa suit ready for another afternoon of being jolly. He drained his coffee and stood, bracing himself like the professional he was.

He'd never felt less fucking jolly in his life.

TWELVE

On Saturday morning, Theo managed to sleep in later than usual. He tended to wake early, programmed into it from the days when he had Archie who was always up with the lark. But after staying up late to watch a film—while checking his phone hopefully every few minutes to see if he had any messages from Luke—he'd slept surprisingly well.

Rolling over with a yawn, Theo reached automatically for his phone, and disappointment punched him in the gut when he saw there was still nothing from Luke.

The morning after their last date, Theo had woken up feeling excited and hopeful. Things had been a little awkward after they'd had sex, but wasn't that often the case with someone new? By the time they'd said their goodbyes Luke seemed fine again and had said he wanted to see Theo again.

But Theo's attempt to arrange another date had met with no success so far. Something had changed. Luke was being slower to reply to his messages, and not very talkative even when he did. He'd mentioned being busy more than once, but Theo suspected it was an excuse. As far as he knew Luke's schedule hadn't changed, and he'd always made time to talk to Theo before. Luke was keeping him at a distance, and Theo didn't understand why.

This morning he didn't bother to send Luke a text to say hello. He was fed up of the long delays and feeling like he was the one making all the effort.

Ignoring his phone, he ate his breakfast in front of the television, and then got dressed ready to go and pick up Archie. He already knew what he was doing today, because he'd spoken to Archie on FaceTime last night. Archie had informed him that Mr Purple and Mrs Blue wanted to go on the train, and then they wanted to visit Santa. He'd sounded very definite about it, and Theo didn't have the heart to argue.

Despondent about the way things had soured with Luke, and gloomy at the prospect of a lonely Christmas Day while Archie was off playing happy families with Caroline and Daniel, Theo needed all the Christmas spirit he could get. Maybe another trip to Santa's Grotto would cheer him up. Archie's happiness was infectious, and the simple pleasure he took in getting a cuddly toy from some bloke dressed in a red padded suit with a ridiculous beard was bound to make Theo smile.

"TRAIN FIRST OR SANTA FIRST?" Theo asked as he pulled into a parking space at the shopping mall. He'd made sure to get there early as it was the last Saturday before Christmas, so it would be rammed later.

"Hmm...." Theo glanced at him in his mirror, and smiled to himself when he saw Archie's frown of concentration as he pondered this very important question.

"How about we do the train first," Theo suggested.

"Then Santa. Because you already have lots to carry, and Santa will give you another present."

Archie had insisted on bringing Mr Purple and Mrs Blue, as well as a plastic stegosaurus—the current favourite of his dinosaur collection.

"Okay," Archie said.

Theo got out and helped Archie out of his car seat. "Do you want me to carry one?"

Archie considered this for a moment. "You can take Mr Purple."

Off they went to buy their tickets for the train. Theo only felt slightly silly carrying a stuffed purple elephant as Archie trotted along beside him. It went with the whole Dad territory so he was used to it.

BY THE TIME they got into Santa's Grotto it was early afternoon. They'd been on the train, and gone to McDonald's for lunch—a rare treat for Archie. Archie was busy colouring in a picture of a sleigh and reindeer, his stegosaurus standing on the table as though watching him. He was utterly absorbed in the task, so Theo got out his phone for the first time in hours. When he saw he had a message from Luke his heart gave a little flip of excitement that Theo quickly tried to squash. He'd already made the mistake of getting his hopes up over Luke once; he didn't want to do it again. Determined to play it cool, he opened his phone.

Luke: Sorry I've been quiet. Work's a bit manic at the moment. Hope all is well with you and that we can meet again after Christmas.

Well that was more positive. At least he was mentioning meeting up again. Theo replied: *Yes I'd like that. And I'm okay. Busy with stuff too.* He pressed send, then let his finger hover over the keyboard, considering. Initially he'd planned to tell Luke about Archie face-to-face on Wednesday, but he'd chickened out. Perhaps it would be easier to do it by text? He started to type: *Actually, there's something you should probably know about me....*

"Daddy, Daddy!" Theo tugged on his sleeve excitedly. "That's our number!"

The elf assistant was standing expectantly by the door to Santa's area. "Number forty-six? Are you here?"

"Yes." Theo stood, holding up his hand. "Coming." He deleted the message he'd started. He'd write it later when he had more time to think about how to approach the subject.

Archie ran over to the elf, stegosaurus in hand. Theo scooped up Mr Purple and Mrs Blue, who he'd had in his lap, and followed Archie through to see Santa.

"Hello, hello, hello," Santa boomed in his jolliest tone. "Well I never. Fancy seeing you here again, Archie."

"You remembered my name!" Archie said.

"Well of course. I don't get many children who come back a third time."

"Do you remember my daddy's name?"

Santa's blue gaze flashed to Theo and settled there. It was impossible to tell what he looked like under the padded suit, with the huge beard and moustache, and the cap that covered his hair and most of his forehead. But from the lack of lines around his eyes, Theo thought he was younger than he'd first suspected.

"Theo, isn't it?" Santa asked.

"That's impressive. Hello again." Theo gave him an awkward smile, surprised that the bloke had remembered his name as well as Archie's.

"Who have you brought to visit me today?" Santa asked as Archie moved in close beside him.

"A stegosaurus." Archie held it up. "And Daddy's got Mr Purple and Mrs Blue. They need a new friend."

Santa laughed and it sounded genuine rather than a ho-ho-ho. "I'm sure that can be arranged. Did you want to get a photo again?"

"Yes please," Archie said. "Can you hold Mr Purple and Mrs Blue?"

"Of course." Santa helped Archie onto his knee and then took the toys from Theo.

Theo got out his phone ready to take the photo. "Archie, I can't see your stegosaurus. Do you want him in the picture?"

Archie held the dinosaur up, and Santa leaned down so his head was closer to Archie.

"Smile," Theo said, and his phone clicked as he took a couple of shots.

"Can I see?" Archie moved quickly, jumping down from Santa's knee eager to see the picture.

"Ouch!" Santa yelped. "You've got my beard." He clutched at his face, but he was too slow. The beard, tangled in the stegosaurus's spikes, came with Archie, leaving Santa with a bare face, aside from a much shorter well-trimmed dark beard of his own.

"Oh, God. I'm so s—" Theo began, but then he froze, staring at Santa. Surely it couldn't be? He blinked in shock for a moment. Then embarrassment and anger poured in, a twisted uncomfortable blend of emotion, making his face heat, and his heart pound. "Luke. What the hell?"

Luke stared back, blue eyes wide as his hands flew up to cover his face.

"Who's Luke?" Archie asked. When neither of them

answered, he untangled the beard and handed it back to Luke, who quickly stuck it back on his face haphazardly, the moustache hanging off on one side. He didn't take his eyes off Theo the whole time, and Theo was stuck staring at him too.

"Daddy, can I see the photo?"

Theo handed Archie his phone wordlessly. His head was reeling. Luke had known all this time. He'd known Theo had a kid, he'd met them twice, and never said. *Why?* Theo wasn't sure whether to be mortified at being caught out in his own dishonesty, or furious with Luke for not telling Theo that he already knew. There were so many things he wanted to say, but he couldn't. Not with Archie there.

"Come on, Archie, we need to hurry. I want to get home to cook tea." Theo dragged his gaze away from Luke. This was awkward as fuck and he needed to escape. "Get your present from Santa, and we'll go."

"Oh, yeah. Of course." The fake Santa voice was gone now, that was all Luke. He rummaged around in his sack and held out a present. Was it Theo's imagination, or was his hand trembling as Archie took it?

"Thank you." Archie unwrapped it immediately like last time, and smiled in delight when he saw a green monkey.

"You're welcome," Luke said, his voice a little strained. "Have a good Christmas, Archie. I hope you have fun with your mum," then he added pointedly, "and that your dad isn't too lonely without you for the day."

Fuck.

Theo's face burned even hotter as he remembered discussing Christmas last time they were here. Then he'd fibbed about his plans to Luke on their date. He felt like such a fucking idiot. Luke must think he was a pathological liar. No wonder he'd been a bit weird since Wednesday. But Theo wasn't the only one keeping secrets. Surely any normal person would have told Theo he'd seen him with his kid? All Luke had to do was mention it in a message later that day and it would have been out in the open.

"I'll cope," Theo managed, his throat tight with anger and discomfort. "Come on, Archie. Let's go."

"Don't forget Mr Purple and Mrs Blue," Luke said. Theo took them from Luke's hands, hating the thrill he got when their fingers touched. Then Luke grabbed his wrist before he could pull away. "I'm sorry," he muttered quietly so Archie wouldn't hear. "I'll text you when I finish work."

He released Theo, who simply said, "Your beard's still hanging off." Then he turned and hurried away, grabbing Archie's hand as he went.

"Bye, Santa," Archie said.

"Bye, Archie. Happy Christmas." Luke was back to using his Santa voice, but his jolly tone had a hollow edge to it.

THIRTEEN

"Fuck, fuck, fuck." Luke muttered under his breath as he watched Theo and Archie's retreating forms. "Well that was awkward."

"You ready for the next one?" Jamie asked, popping his head around the door.

"Give me a minute. I need to fix my beard."

"Want a hand? Here, let me." Jamie came up to Luke and pressed the edge of his moustache down. "I think that'll do, what happened?"

My love life just imploded and the first guy I liked in ages probably won't want to speak to me ever again, Luke thought. But aloud he only said, "A stegosaurus."

"Huh?"

Luke gave a heavy sigh. "Hashtag Santa problems. Never mind; it's a long story. Send the next kid in."

AS SOON AS Luke was out of work, he messaged Theo as he walked to the bus stop.

Luke: I'm sorry today was weird. Can we talk about it?

He carried on walking with his phone in his hand, willing it to buzz with a reply. But he didn't get one until he was waiting at the bus stop in the cold.

Theo: Why the hell didn't you tell me you knew about Archie?

Luke frowned. He'd been expecting Theo to be more apologetic than angry with him, and Theo's aggressive tone made Luke defensive.

Luke: Why the hell didn't you tell me you had a kid?

Theo: I would have eventually. It didn't seem relevant to tell you straight away.

Luke: We've been talking for over two weeks now, and met twice.

Theo: We've actually met five times if you count the times you were dressed as a fat man with a white beard :/

Luke snorted with laughter despite himself.

Luke: Yes, okay. Sorry about that. Can I come and see you later? I want to sort this out, if you do. And it would be easier to talk in person.

He waited for an anxious few minutes without a reply. Then his bus turned up, and as he was taking his seat his phone buzzed again.

Theo: Not tonight. I've got Archie here.

Luke: Tomorrow night then?

Theo: I'm working late.

Luke: We can talk on the phone then? Please?

A few minutes passed, then came:

Theo: Sorry, Archie spilt milk all over the kitchen floor. I think I'd prefer to talk face-to-face.

Well that was something. If Theo wanted to see him, Luke reckoned this was still fixable.

Luke: When are you free next?

Theo: Christmas Eve in the afternoon.

That was the day after tomorrow. Not too long to wait, and Luke would be free because it was a Monday. His last day of Santa duty was tomorrow.

Luke: That works for me.

Theo: I'll have Archie with me again though.

Luke: That doesn't bother me.

If he was going to try to make a go of things with Theo, getting to know Archie better couldn't hurt. He was just glad Theo was giving them a chance to work things out.

Theo: Fine. Meet me in St Michael's Park in Broad Leaze at 2 p.m.

Luke: Okay :)

CHRISTMAS EVE WAS BRIGHT, but freezing. When Luke arrived at the park the low winter sun shone in a clear sky, but frost still clung thickly to the blades of grass that had spent the day in shadow.

He got there a little early, because of how the bus times worked, but Theo and Archie were earlier. He spotted them as he approached the fenced off children's area. Theo's red scarf was a vivid splash of colour as he pushed Archie on a toddler swing. Luke smiled when he saw that Archie was holding Mr Purple.

Heart thumping with nerves, Luke went through the gate and as it closed with a clang behind him, Theo looked up, and their eyes met.

There were several other parents and children around, but as Luke locked gazes with Theo the rest of the world seemed to fade away for a moment. Was it Luke's imagination or did Theo's face reflect the hope that burned in Luke's chest?

"Hi," Luke said when he reached them. He offered a

wary smile. Everything felt weird. It was almost like a first date all over again, only worse because they had this stupid mess between them to untangle.

"Hey." Theo's smile was hesitant too.

"Who's this, Daddy?" Archie asked, craning around to look at Luke.

"This is Luke, Archie. Remember I told you a friend of mine was coming to meet us in the park?"

"Oh." Archie eyed him warily, and Luke remembered Archie had been shy with him at first when he was dressed as Santa. He obviously didn't recognise him despite the beard debacle of the day before.

"Hi, Archie." Luke gave his best reassuring smile.

"Hi. Daddy, keep pushing!"

"Sorry, buddy."

Theo got back to it while Luke stood awkwardly next to him. How were they supposed to have this conversation with Archie there? "So, um. How are you?" Luke asked.

"Not bad, thanks. Looking forward to two days off in a row for a change. That doesn't often happen."

"Only two?"

"Yeah, straight back to the grindstone the day after Boxing Day. What about you?"

"Well, I'm done with the Christmas job for now." Luke looked down at his feet, cheeks flushing despite the cold. "And I don't start my new job at the pharmacy till January."

"All right for some." There was an uncomfortable pause. "So, are you looking forward to your mum's Christmas dinner tomorrow?"

Luke swallowed. "Um. About that...." He raised his eyes to meet Theo's. "I'm not really going to my mum's. I'm actually on my own tomorrow too."

Theo lifted an eyebrow. "You lied about your Christmas plans too?"

"You started it. And you used the phrase 'lonely saddo' if I recall correctly. I was hardly going to admit to my lack of plans after that. Even if spending Christmas alone was actually my choice. My stepdad is a pain in the arse so I'll have more fun binge-watching *Game of Thrones* and eating supermarket pizza."

"Yeah, that doesn't sound too bad." Theo's lips curved in a faint smile.

"Can I get down now, Daddy?" Archie asked.

"Course." Theo held the swing still while Archie scrambled out.

"Mr Purple wants to go on the slide." Mr Purple in hand, he ran off towards the play equipment—a wooden frame with various nets and ladders, with a large slide at one end.

They watched for a moment as Archie started to climb. He seemed absorbed, and happy to be on his own.

"Want to sit down?" Theo gestured to a bench.

"Sure."

They sat side by side, but with a distance between them that was mental as well as physical. Luke wanted to shuffle closer, or take Theo's hand. But he wasn't sure Theo would want that, and not just because they were in public.

"So, why didn't you tell me about Archie?" Luke was still hurt by the deception. Archie was obviously a really important part of Theo's life. Judging by the amount of time they seemed to spend together, Theo must have done a lot of lying by omission when he'd talked about his days.

"I would have told you eventually," Theo said. "But I wanted to get to know you better first. I was afraid it might put you off. You said something a bit negative about kids in one of our first chats."

"I did?" Luke frowned. "But I like kids! What did I say?"

"Something about your niece and nephew being hard work and how you were glad you'd never have any of your own... or that was the gist of it anyway."

Luke vaguely remembered it now, and wished he could take those words back. "It was a throwaway comment. I was trying to be funny. Fuck. I love my niece and nephew. I have to admit I've never really thought about having kids of my own, but knowing about Archie wouldn't have stopped me wanting to date you."

"Well if it had, you wouldn't be the first guy who lost interest when he found out. And I didn't want Archie to be the reason that we never even tried."

"Okay. I guess I can see why you might have waited."

"So, why didn't you tell me when you found out?" Theo turned to him, and Luke met his gaze. His eyes were intense, the bright winter sky highlighting flecks of green and gold. "I felt like such a fucking idiot when I realised you knew all the time."

"I'm sorry. But I did what I thought was best at the time," Luke said earnestly. "It was obvious you weren't ready to tell me about Archie, so I was trying to respect that. I wasn't trying to catch you out, or trick you. I was hoping that eventually you'd trust me and would tell me you had a kid. Then I would have admitted that I already knew, and told you how. I thought we'd be able to laugh about it eventually." He stared at Theo, willing him to understand.

When Theo's face relaxed into a small smile, Luke's shoulders dropped, the tension melting away like ice in the sun.

"Maybe we will." Theo's smile widened. "It was pretty funny that your beard got pulled off by Archie's stegosaurus. If it hadn't been you under there I'd have struggled to keep a straight face."

Luke huffed. "Well I'm glad it was funny for you. It fucking hurt! He nearly took my real beard with it."

Theo's lips twitched, and then he chuckled. "Sorry, sorry. But it *was* funny."

Luke laughed. "I guess it was. Santa unmasked by a dinosaur. That's not something you see every day." They grinned at each other, and Luke's heart lifted with hope. "Are we good now?"

Theo nodded. "Yeah. We're good."

His lips were pink and there were dimples on his cheeks. Luke ached to touch him and kiss him, but he couldn't. Not with Archie there. Instead he said quietly, "I really want to kiss you right now."

Flushing, Theo looked over at Archie, then back to Luke. "Yeah. I wish you could too. But we can't. Not here."

"I know." Instead Luke settled for shuffling closer on the bench until their knees touched. "Is this okay though?"

Theo shuffled closer still, pressing their thighs together, and putting an arm along the back of the bench. "Definitely."

They sat in silence for a moment. But all the wariness of before had gone. Now it was a comfortable silence, edged with anticipation. With the dishonesty and misunderstandings of the past behind them, the future looked as bright as the winter sun that slanted through the bare branches of the trees at the edge of the park.

Archie had made a friend, a girl who looked a little older than him. They were playing on the roundabout together, taking it in turns to push each other as her mother looked on. Luke caught the woman's eye and she smiled at him. He returned her smile to be polite, but wasn't quite sure what he'd done to earn it.

"So...." Theo let his arm slip off the back of the bench to rest on Luke's shoulder. "As things stand, we're both spending Christmas Day alone."

"Apparently." Luke glanced sideways to see a smile tugging at the corners of Theo's mouth.

"That seems like the universe is trying to tell us something."

"Does it?" Luke asked innocently.

"Unless of course you would rather watch *Game of Thrones* alone all day. Far be it from me to cramp your style...."

"Well. I suppose you could come over, and we could watch it together. Do you like pizza?"

Theo chuckled. "It wouldn't be my first choice on Christmas Day, but I'm easy."

"It's a date then."

"Yes." Theo's smile warmed Luke from his head to his toes. "Our fourth—if today counts?"

"Hmm. I'm not sure whether sitting in a park and having a conversation counts as a date. Maybe if we go to a cafe for some sort of hot beverage after this, then it might qualify."

"That sounds good to me, and Archie will never say no to hot chocolate."

"Daddy!" Archie called from the swing. "Can you push again?"

"Speak of the devil." Theo stood, and Luke missed the weight of his arm on his shoulder as soon as it was gone. He got up and followed Theo over to the swings.

Archie was on one of the big kid swings this time, trying

to hold onto the chains and Mr Purple at the same time. His new friend was in the swing next to him, and she'd already got it moving. "Look, it's easy," she said. "Just swing your legs and lean like this."

"Daddy, help." Archie was pink in the face with frustration.

"Give me Mr Purple, Arch. You need to hold on properly."

"I'll take him," Luke offered.

Archie handed him over. "Hold him so he can see me swing."

"Okay." Luke did as instructed, feeling slightly foolish as he stood in front of the swings, just out of reach of the arc.

The mother of the girl wandered over and stood next to him. "They've been playing so nicely for ages," she said.

"Yeah," Luke agreed vaguely. He hadn't actually been paying much attention to what Archie was doing. His focus had been on Theo.

"He's a lovely little boy," she said. "You and your partner must be very proud of him."

"Um," Luke faltered as his brain whirled for a moment, surprised by how good it felt to be mistaken for a family. "We're not... I mean.... He's not my partner as such. We're just dating. Archie is his son."

"Oh, I see." She was unfazed. "Well you look very happy together."

Luke smiled. "Yeah, well. It's early days. But I hope it's going somewhere."

AS THEY SAT in a cosy cafe a little later, drinking coffees —and hot chocolate for Archie—Luke found himself looking around at the other customers, wondering how many of them would make the same assumption as the lady in the park. Was it weird that he found himself almost hoping that people would think they were a family? Having a kid had never been part of Luke's life plan, but actually it would be pretty amazing to be a stepdad. He was damn sure he'd be much better at it than his own stepfather.

"Are you excited about Christmas tomorrow, Archie?" he asked.

"Yes." Archie grinned, a whipped cream moustache on his upper lip. "I'll get to see Santa again. In Mummy's house this time!"

Theo flashed a worried look at Luke. "I'm not sure you will, buddy. Santa comes while you're asleep. So you won't get to see him again this year."

Archie's face fell. "I won't see him?" Theo shook his head. "But I like talking to him. He's nice."

"He doesn't have time to stop and talk on Christmas Day, Archie. Because he has to deliver toys to all the other boys and girls," Theo was babbling now, but his words didn't help. Archie's blue eyes were filling with tears.

Suddenly Luke was hit by a stroke of genius. "Maybe he can come and see you at your daddy's house on Boxing Day though. If that's okay with your dad?"

Theo stared at him, eyebrows raised.

Luke winked, and continued. "I reckon he'll be less busy that day, so maybe he can pop by and say hello—if he's invited."

Archie gave a wobbly smile. "He'll come and see me there?"

Luke nodded. "Yes. Santa's a mate of mine, so I'll let him know you're expecting him."

Theo was looking at Luke incredulously, but Luke gave

him a confident smile and a thumbs up. He could make this happen. He needed to go back to the mall before it shut later to buy a present for Theo anyway, and some food for tomorrow—something other than pizza now he had a guest —so it would be no trouble to go back to work and borrow his Santa suit. They wouldn't be needing it again for a while.

When Archie got bored of sitting at the table with them and got down to play with the toys in the corner set aside for kids, Theo asked, "Did you mean it? You can dress up in the suit and come over?"

"If you want," Luke said, suddenly worried he'd over-stepped. They hadn't even spent Christmas together yet and he'd basically gatecrashed Theo's day with Archie. "I can pop over for an hour or so."

"That would be brilliant." Theo grinned. "Yes please."

FOURTEEN

Theo's spirits were high as he drove over to Luke's on Christmas morning. The prospect of spending Christmas with Luke had made it easier to say goodbye to Archie when he dropped him off at Caroline's last night. He'd had a quiet evening and an early night, and woke fresh and full of excitement at the day ahead.

He passed a small supermarket that was open, despite the date, and the sight of it reminded him that he hadn't got Luke anything for Christmas. *Bollocks.* He should have thought of that yesterday when there were more shops to choose from. But he wouldn't have wanted to drag Archie to the mall in the insanity of last minute Christmas Eve panic buying. Luke probably hadn't had time to get him anything either, but as Luke was hosting, Theo didn't want to turn up empty handed.

After pulling over, he hurried back to the shop. It was a typical small supermarket and newsagent, selling mainly food and drink, plus a few household bits and pieces. There was very little that would make an interesting Christmas gift, but Theo reckoned he couldn't go wrong with booze and chocolates. If things went well today, then maybe he could get Luke a belated gift for next time they met.

Theo picked up a box of Quality Street and a bottle of champagne and took them to the till.

"Hello, merry Christmas," said the man behind the counter.

"Thanks, you too." Theo paid for his items, and said yes to a carrier bag in lieu of wrapping paper.

AS HE PULLED up outside Luke's flat, Theo's heart kicked up a notch. He pressed the bell, and Luke's voice crackled through the intercom. "Hi?"

"Hey, it's me."

"Come on up." The door buzzed, and as Theo pushed, it opened. He hurried up the stairs to find Luke waiting for him in his flat doorway with a huge smile on his face. Wearing jeans and a dark red shirt, his hair still damp from the shower, Luke looked gorgeous. The sight of him made heat flare in Theo's belly.

Theo walked straight into his arms, curling his free hand around the nape of Luke's neck and they kissed each other softly.

"Sorry I'm a little bit late," Theo said when they separated. "I stopped at a shop on the way."

"It's only five past eleven." Luke grinned. "I was impatient to see you, but I think I can let you off five minutes. Come in." He stepped back through the open door and guided Theo inside.

"Happy Christmas," Theo said, offering him the bag. "Sorry it's not very exciting, but this was all a bit last minute."

"Oh thank you." Luke peered in. "Yum. I love Quality

Street, and champagne too, awesome. I'd better get that in the fridge for later—or the freezer in case we want it soon."

Theo followed him into the kitchen.

"What do you want now?" Luke asked. "Tea, coffee, beer, wine?"

"Just a glass of water is fine." Theo was hoping Luke would be up for some fun early in the day, and he wanted to keep a clear head so he could enjoy it.

Luke poured glasses for both of them, and they took them through to the living room. "Sorry it's not very festive," Luke said. "I didn't have time to sort out a tree or anything. But I managed to pick up some tinsel in the shops last night and the fairy lights were on special offer. It was a bit of a rush job." He gestured to the mantelpiece where silver and gold tinsel was draped over the top of it, and a string of fairy lights was stuck up with sellotape.

Theo grinned. "It looks nice. Thanks for bothering. But I'm here to see you, not judge you on your Christmas decorations." He sidled over to Luke, took the glass out of his hand, and put both their drinks down on the coffee table. With those out of the way, he toed his shoes off, then pushed Luke down to sit on the sofa, straddled him and kissed him again. It started tentative, like a question. But Luke put his hands on Theo's hips and moaned into the kiss, opening his mouth, inviting more. Theo pulled away, chuckling as a thought occurred to him.

"What's so funny?" Luke asked.

"I'm sitting in Santa's lap."

Luke laughed, and then wiggled his eyebrows suggestively. "Have you been a good boy?"

"Yes. Very good." Theo ground down against Luke, dipping his head to kiss him again.

Luke hummed, reaching to stroke Theo through his

jeans, thumbing the head of his cock where he was hard and pushing against the fabric. He moved to kiss Theo's neck, licking the skin and making Theo gasp. "You feel pretty naughty to me. And this reminds me. I bought you a present too."

"Yeah?" Theo didn't care about presents right now. He wanted more kissing, and less clothes between them. He rubbed against Luke again, pleased to feel that he was hard as well. "Show me later."

"Actually, I think you might appreciate it now."

Something in Luke's tone made Theo stop and pay attention. He drew back so he could see Luke's suggestive grin. "Oh yes?"

Luke slapped him on the arse. "Let me up, and I'll go and get it."

Theo climbed off him and sat back on the sofa, adjusting his cock while Luke went into his bedroom.

He came out with his hands behind his back. "Close your eyes and open your hands."

"Not my mouth?" Theo smirked.

Luke snorted. "You really are a naughty boy aren't you? Or good, depending on your definition. Hands."

Theo obeyed, shutting his eyes, and opening his palms.

Luke placed something in them. It was quite heavy, and rustled as Theo felt the shape of it. It was curved, like the top of an old fashioned walking stick. "Can I look now?"

"Sure, and you can open it too."

Theo opened his eyes, and tore into the paper, impatient to see what Luke had got him. Once he had it open, he was still none the wiser. Made of clear glass with red and white spirals wrapping around it, the mystery gift was about nine inches long with a slight bulb on each end, and was thick enough that he could just wrap his fingers around it.

Theo held it up so the light shone through it. "It's pretty, but what is it?"

"It's a candy cane." Luke grinned, expectantly.

"But not one I can eat. So, what's it for?"

Luke got his other hand out from behind his back and handed Theo a second gift. This one was smaller, and shaped like a bottle.

When Theo tore the paper off, his eyes widened. "Oh." It was a bottle of lube. Suddenly the first gift made sense. "Wow. Thank you."

"I hope you like it," Luke said. "I mostly got it as a joke, but you said you're versatile so I thought you might have fun with it."

"I will." Theo put the lube down and stroked the long end of the dildo. "God. I bet it will feel amazing, that bulb at the end, and the way the red and white parts are ridged."

"Yeah?" Luke's voice was husky, and when Theo met his gaze his eyes were dark and he licked his lips. "Bet you'd look hot using it too. Maybe you can send me a picture."

"I've got a better idea," Theo said. "How about you use it on me now? Then you can see for yourself how much fun I have with it."

Luke's eyes lit up. "Seriously?"

"Mmhmm." Theo spread his legs wider and reached down to rub the bulge in his jeans. "I want you to fuck me with it, and then fuck me with your cock."

"I can do that." Luke pushed the coffee table aside, and knelt between Theo's knees. Theo leaned forward to kiss him as Luke started work on his fly. "Lift up," Luke said between kisses, and he helped Theo out of his jeans and underwear. "Cute socks."

Theo grinned. "Seemed appropriate." He stretched out

his legs, showing off the dark green socks with little Santas all over them.

Luke moved back up to kiss him, one hand going to Theo's cock as the other reached lower. Theo shuffled forward to give Luke better access, and moaned into the kiss as Luke rubbed a finger lightly over his hole. The idea of Luke working the dildo into him had him wound tight already.

"You're so eager." Luke murmured, nipping his neck.

"Yep." Theo reached for the lube which was slipping down the crack between the sofa cushions. "Here." He pressed it into Luke's hand.

As Luke sat back and squeezed some lube onto his fingers, Theo took off his jumper. It was warm in Luke's flat and his whole body felt flushed and hot, his skin prickling with the sweat of arousal. He stripped his T-shirt off too, tossing them both aside.

"I feel a little overdressed." Luke smiled, his gaze roaming approvingly over Theo. "God, you look hot like that though. Naked, and waiting for me to play with you."

Theo's cock jerked at his words, precome smearing on his stomach. "Not quite naked." He grinned, lifting his feet, and wiggling his toes. "You still being fully dressed is kind of a turn on too, though. It makes me feel extra naughty."

"Yeah. I get that." Luke started to stroke Theo's hole again, his slippery finger tracing an insistent circle. Theo moaned and reached for his cock, but Luke batted his hand away and guided him into his mouth instead. As he slid his lips around the crown, he pushed a finger into Theo, making him gasp at the dual sensations as Luke moved his finger and sucked on his cock.

"Fuck, that's good." Theo squeezed around Luke's finger. "Give me another one."

Luke obliged, working two in and twisting them, he sucked Theo deeper. He carried on doing that for a little while, the wet sounds of his mouth and fingers turning Theo on even more. Eventually Luke pulled off, his fingers still inside, and said, "You ready to try your present?"

"Definitely," Theo said, a little breathless now. Luke withdrew his fingers, and lubed up the dildo. He took his time, and Theo licked his lips as he watched the slow movement of Luke's hand, deliberately suggestive as he rubbed the lube up and over the thick bulb at the tip. "Hurry up."

"I'm just warming it up for you. The glass is cold."

"I don't care. It'll warm up soon enough." Theo squirmed on the sofa, empty and impatient to be filled.

The first touch of it was cold, but the contrast with the heat of his body felt amazing to Theo. There was resistance, as Luke worked it into him, but once the bulb was inside, the rest slid in easily and Theo groaned at the feeling of the ridges and the pressure of the thick head nudging against his prostate.

"You look amazing," Luke said. His gaze raked over Theo and zeroed in on his hole. "So fucking hot. Oh my God." He unbuttoned his jeans one-handed and his erection stuck out, stretching the fabric of his pale grey underwear. A dark spot bloomed at the tip. "Look how wet you made me."

Theo whimpered, torn between the desire to have Luke's cock in his mouth and taste him, and the need to be fucked. "I want to suck you." He got a hand down to the dildo. "Let me do this for a minute. Get up here and give me your cock."

Luke scrambled up, not pausing to take off any clothes. He knelt beside Theo on the sofa, and Theo shuffled down so his mouth was level with that tempting bulge. He licked it, tasting precome through the fabric, and Luke slid a hand into his hair and groaned. "Fuck, Theo. Here... let me...." He freed his cock with his other hand and guided it to Theo's lips, sliding it back and forth, slippery and wet, until Theo opened his mouth and let Luke push inside. Theo hummed his pleasure, sucking and swirling his tongue as he fucked the dildo into himself. His own cock was achingly hard, but he resisted the urge to stroke himself, afraid he'd come if he did. Instead he used his free hand to cup Luke's balls, squeezing and tugging gently as he sucked.

"Fuck, Theo." Luke broke away panting. "Time out. Otherwise I'm gonna come."

Theo grinned at him and reached up, guiding him down for a kiss instead. "I'm close too," he said between wet hungry kisses. "Won't take much. Do you want to fuck me?"

"Yeah. We'll need to move though. The condoms are in my room. Come on."

Luke stood, picking up the lube. Theo let the dildo slip out of him, clenching on nothing once it was gone. Luke offered him a hand up and led him to his bedroom.

"What position do you fancy?" Theo asked as Luke stripped his clothes off.

"On your back. I want to be able to kiss you."

Theo spread himself out on his back, the dildo cast aside. It was fun while it lasted but he wanted Luke inside him. He watched, stroking his dick slowly as Luke rolled on a condom and slathered it with lube. "Hurry up," Theo said. "Want your cock."

"Hope it feels enough after that dildo." Luke eyed it doubtfully. "Maybe I should have bought a smaller one."

"Don't be daft." Theo opened his legs wider and reached for Luke as he lowered himself between Theo's thighs. "The dildo was great, but you're better because you're you. I want you to come in me. A dildo can't do that."

Luke guided his cock to Theo's hole and slid inside easily. He wasn't as big as the dildo but he was warm and hard and he felt amazing. As Luke lowered himself for a hungry kiss, Theo's cock was trapped between their stomachs and he arched into the touch as Luke thrust into him with steady, devastating strokes. The angle was perfect, Theo was so close already, it wasn't going to take long if Luke carried on like that.

"Want me to jerk you off?" Luke murmured against Theo's throat before kissing it. "Or do you want to do it yourself?"

"Don't need it, not if you carry on doing that. Stay close, it feels so good."

Luke groaned. "God, that's hot. I want to make you come just by fucking you."

"Yeah. Don't stop." Luke thrust harder and faster. The rest of the world slipped away as Theo got closer and closer to that perfect edge. All he was aware of was Luke's mouth on his neck, warm skin touching him everywhere, the scratch and tickle of Luke's hairy chest on his nipples, the friction against this dick, and the glorious pressure and stretch of Luke's cock inside him. "Fuck. Coming," Theo gasped, body tensing as he started to shoot, hot and slippery between them.

"Me too." Luke thrust in balls deep, hips flexing. Theo grabbed his arse, pulling him close, and keeping him there as the last pulses of his orgasm faded. Knowing that Luke was coming too was so hot. He wished there wasn't a condom between them. "Fuck," Luke said breathlessly, lifting his face from Theo's neck and grinning. He looked totally blissed out. "That was awesome."

"Yeah." Theo grinned too, sure that his smile was as dazed as Luke's. His body was still alight with pleasure, nerve endings tingling as his heart slowed and settled.

Luke pulled out and knotted and tossed the condom, then lay beside Theo with his arm over his chest. Theo turned his head for a kiss. "Happy Christmas."

"Hell yes it is." Luke chuckled. "This definitely beats spending it alone."

FIFTEEN

Luke let Theo rinse off in the shower first, although they were both equally sticky from where Theo had come all over them. While Theo was in there, Luke went naked into the kitchen and put the oven on to pre-heat. Sex had given him an appetite; hopefully it would have had the same effect on Theo.

"Well that's quite a sight." Theo's amused voice made Luke turn to see him in the kitchen doorway. "Although you should probably wear an apron to protect your dick. Health and safety."

Luke laughed. "Don't worry. I'll cover up before I put anything in the oven."

"What are we having?"

"I got snack food for lunch—mini samosas and onion bhajis and stuff like that. I thought we'd have the big meal this evening. I ended up getting turkey and other traditional stuff instead of pizza. Hope that's okay with you?"

"That's perfect. Can I help with anything now?" Theo's gaze slid down to Luke's cock.

"No. I think I'm good. But maybe you can give me a hand with something later," Luke said.

"I'm sure I can." Theo gave him a mischievous grin.

"Right. I'll go and clean up and get some clothes back on. Help yourself to anything in the meantime. There's beer and wine in the fridge, or we could open the champagne? I put it in the freezer so it should be cold by now."

"That sounds perfect."

"Glasses are in that cupboard." Luke pointed. "I'll only be a few minutes."

When Luke emerged clean, dry, and dressed, he found Theo in the living room on the sofa, glasses and the champagne waiting on the coffee table. "Do you want to do the honours?" Theo asked.

"Sure."

Luke popped the cork and filled two glasses. He handed a glass to Theo who raised it, smiling. "Cheers."

"Cheers." Luke clinked carefully and they both took a sip. The bubbles fizzed on Luke's tongue, and it was ice cold and delicious. "Oh that's lush. Thanks so much for bringing it."

"Thanks for inviting me. Well... I guess I almost invited myself."

Luke grinned. "I was going to ask you anyway, so you saved me the trouble." His stomach growled loudly, reminding him it was lunchtime. "I'll go and get the snacks into the oven."

LUKE HAD SPLASHED out at Marks and Spencer and bought the turkey crown and all the trimmings and vegetables pre-prepared so there wasn't much cooking to do for dinner.

As a result, the afternoon passed in a blissfully relaxed haze of alcohol, and all the things about Christmas that Luke liked: chilling in front of the TV, playing Monopoly, and none of the stuff he hated: like having to peel sprouts, being on his best behaviour, and putting up with his stepdad being a twat.

"That turkey smells amazing," Theo said.

They were stretched out on the sofa, Theo behind Luke, his arms around him as they watched *Elf*. It was amazing how natural it felt having Theo here. Luke had to keep reminding himself they'd only been on a couple of dates. He was a little worried about how attached he was getting, but he couldn't have stopped himself even if he'd wanted to. Theo was such easy company; he was fun to be around, and relaxed, and affectionate. Luke's heart fluttered dangerously whenever Theo smiled at him.

"Yeah." Luke checked his watch. "It must be nearly time to get the veg on, the timer will go any minute I reckon."

Theo kissed the side of his neck, making Luke melt again, and murmured, "Good. I'm hungry," in a way that made Luke think about a totally different kind of appetite.

Sure enough, a minute or so later the shrill beep of the oven timer meant he had to tear himself away from his comfy spot, and away from Theo.

"Need me to do things?" Theo asked, yawning.

"Uh. You could lay the table I guess?" There was a small table by the window in the living room. Luke and Charlie normally ate off their laps on the sofa, but for a special occasion eating at the table seemed like the right thing to do. "Sorry, it's covered in crap. You can dump that on the coffee table for now."

He left Theo gathering up magazines and unopened mail, and went to the kitchen to put the carrots and green beans on to steam. Then he returned to the living room with cutlery.

"Have you got any candles?" Theo asked.

"I don't think so...." Luke frowned, wishing he'd thought of that when he was shopping yesterday. "Oh, Charlie does though. They're in her room but I'm sure she won't mind if we borrow them." He went into Charlie's room, which was a complete tip. Sure enough, lined up on her dressing table were several tea light candles in glass holders. They'd already burned down a little, but would do for an hour while they had dinner. There was a box of matches next to them, so he put that in his pocket and picked up three of the candles.

"Here." Luke set them down on the table. "I'd better go and start carving. And do you want wine with dinner?"

"I probably shouldn't if I'm going to drive back later," Theo said. "The champagne will wear off in time for me to drive home, but if I top it up with wine I'll be over the limit."

"You can stay here. Sorry, I should have said earlier." Luke could have kicked himself for not making the invitation explicit. He'd just assumed Theo would want to stay. "If you want to that is? No pressure." He tried to keep his tone light, but inside he was begging Theo to say yes.

"Yeah?" Theo looked thoughtful. "I guess I could, if that's okay with you? As long as I get home early tomorrow for Archie. In that case, I'd love some wine. Thanks."

"Cool," Luke said, turning away to hide his elated grin. When he was out of sight in the kitchen he couldn't resist doing a little fist pump before getting started on carving and serving.

By the time he'd dished up the food, Theo had joined

him in the kitchen again and he carried red wine and glasses through while Luke carried their plates.

Luke paused in the doorway to the living room. "Oh wow, that looks fantastic."

Theo had turned off the overhead light, leaving a side lamp on in the corner, and the fairy lights over the mantelpiece. The candles on the table cast a warm flickering glow, and the usual clutter of the room was muted in shadow, making it seem cosy and intimate.

At the table, they sat opposite each other and raised their glasses of red.

"Cheers, happy Christmas." Theo's eyes glittered in the candlelight and his smile made warmth bloom in Luke's chest.

"It really is," Luke replied, holding his gaze. His voice came out with a rough edge when he added, "I'm glad you're here."

Theo didn't hesitate. "I'm glad I'm here too."

AFTER THEY'D EATEN and cleared away. Luke made a duty call to his mum, while Theo phoned to speak to Archie. Theo's call took much longer than Luke's; Archie clearly had lots to tell him. When Theo finally ended the call he was smiling wistfully.

"You okay?" Luke moved closer and put a hand on Theo's thigh.

"Yeah. I just miss him. It's silly. I know I don't normally see him every day anyway, but somehow today...."

"I get it." Luke squeezed his leg, and Theo covered Luke's hand with his own.

"Thanks." He kissed Luke's cheek. "So, about tomorrow. Are you really okay to dress up as Santa for Archie?"

"Yes, of course, if you want me to?"

"It would be amazing, and totally make his day." Theo beamed, and Luke's heart flipped. He'd do pretty much anything to make Theo smile like that at him. "Do you want to come straight over to my place with me when I drive back tomorrow? Caroline is dropping Archie off at ten, so maybe you could be in the suit when he arrives?"

"Or I could hide, and then sneak out and ring on the doorbell so it looks like I'm just visiting," Luke suggested.

"Oh yes, that would be even better. Then you could stash the suit in my car and come back as you, and he won't make the connection. I'm not ready for him to stop believing in Santa yet."

"If you want... I mean, if you want me to come back? I thought you'd want me to head off after that, leave you and Archie in peace."

Theo flushed, lowering his gaze to where their hands were still joined. "Actually, I'd really like you to stay and hang out with us for a while—if you'd like to? Of course if you've got other stuff to do that's fine. Maybe it's the last thing you feel like doing after working with kids for the last month. Sorry I should have thought—"

"I'd love to." Luke picked up Theo's hand and threaded their fingers together. "Anyway. If we're going to carry on dating it would be good to have a chance to get to know Archie better, and for him to get to know me as Luke rather than as Santa."

Theo's face lit up into a smile. "Exactly."

THEY SPENT the evening snuggling on the sofa, trading kisses, finishing the bottle of red, and watching Christmas movies. Eventually Theo started to yawn.

"Sorry," he said, rubbing his eyes. "I woke up early this morning even though Archie wasn't there. My body clock tends to kick in regardless."

"That's okay," Luke said. "I'm ready for bed too."

"Have you got a spare toothbrush?" Theo asked.

"Yeah, in the bathroom cabinet. They were on buy two get one free so I stocked up. Help yourself."

"Thanks."

While Theo used the bathroom, Luke turned off the TV and the fairy lights and made sure that all the leftovers were in the fridge. Then he took his turn. By the time he got to his room, Theo was already under the covers.

"I hope you've warmed it up for me," Luke said. It was getting chilly now the heating had gone off for the night.

"Shit, your hands are cold," Theo protested as Luke pulled him into an embrace. They were both dressed only in underwear, but Luke's duvet was thick.

"Sorry. They'll warm up soon." He rubbed Theo's arms and shoulders and moved in to kiss him.

Theo kissed him back, hooking a leg over Luke's thigh to keep them close, and soon they were both toasty warm from their shared body heat.

"Mmm." Luke pressed his hardening cock against the bulge he could feel in Theo's underwear.

Theo snaked a hand down between them, and into Luke's boxer briefs. He curled his fingers around Luke's cock and stroked. Taking his lead from Theo, Luke mirrored his action and they broke the kiss for a moment to push their underwear down and kick it off so they could reach each other better.

It was a little awkward, especially for Luke because he had to use his left hand as he was lying on his right side, and their hands kept bumping each other. But the squeeze and stroke of Theo's hand on his cock soon had Luke wet and slippery with precome. From the huff of Theo's breath and the passion in his kisses, Luke could tell he was getting close to the edge too. Luke came first, moaning into the kiss as his cock spilled into Theo's grip. Theo stroked him through it, kissing him fiercely, and thrusting into Luke's fist until he came too, slicking Luke's fingers, and adding to the mess between them.

They finally parted, breathless, and grinning. "Um... I think we need a tissue. Probably several tissues," Theo said. He released Luke's softening dick and held up his sticky hand.

"I don't have any in here. Ugh. I don't want to get out of bed now I'm all warm." Luke felt around with his foot and managed to snag his boxer briefs from under the covers. "Here, use these."

Theo chuckled, but took them. He wiped his hand first, then his cock, and then handed them to Luke so he could clean up too. "That's kind of hot actually. Our come all mixed together."

"Dirty boy," Luke said teasingly. "But yeah. It is."

They'd got a little on the sheets too, but Luke could ignore the wet patch. He had Theo in his bed, sleepy and smiling at him, and that was all that mattered.

Theo yawned and rolled onto his back, stretching. "I'm knackered now. In the best way."

"Yeah, me too. Shall I turn out the light?"

"Yeah."

Luke hit the switch and plunged them into cosy darkness. Rolling back, he found Theo and wrapped an arm over his chest. "Is this okay? Do you like cuddling while you sleep?"

"I love it." Theo moved again, turning so he was the

little spoon to Luke's big one. He took Luke's hand and stroked it with feather-light circles that made Luke's skin tingle. "This is really great. I had an amazing Christmas. Thank you so much."

Luke's heart swelled. "Same. And it really was my pleasure."

"Night, Luke." Theo's voice was soft at the edges with sleep now.

"Night." Luke pressed a kiss to the warm skin at the nape of Theo's neck and stayed there, breathing in the scent of him until they both drifted into sleep.

SIXTEEN

Theo woke a few times in the night. Being in a strange bed with another person meant he didn't sleep soundly. But every time he woke, he remembered where he was and smiled before dozing off again. Luke was an affectionate sleeper. He always had an arm across Theo, or a hand on his chest or hip, whatever position they ended up in. It felt good, reassuring, and as though Luke was happy that Theo was there.

At half seven, Theo was wide awake and couldn't get back to sleep. He needed a pee, but not enough to leave the warm comfort of Luke's bed and risk disturbing Luke who was the little spoon now. Theo was curved around his back, his arm around Luke's hairy chest. So Theo lay there and enjoyed the feeling of Luke in his arms, running over the day they'd spent together yesterday, and how perfect it had been.

It felt as though they'd fast forwarded from their tentative start of dating to something special. The initial prevarications and misunderstandings and their subsequent honesty had pushed them into a new closeness. Theo was excited about how things had changed between them and hopeful for the future of their relationship, even though they hadn't talked about what they wanted yet. The way they were when they spent time together made him optimistic that Luke might want something more serious. And Theo thought he could be serious about Luke if he had the chance. Now Luke knew about Archie, that didn't feel like a barrier anymore.

Today would be the litmus test. If Luke spent the day with him and Archie and still wanted to carry on dating after that, then Theo reckoned he was a keeper. His heart fluttered with nerves and anticipation at the thought. Archie was the centre of Theo's world, any man in his life was going to have to be able to deal with that, and it seemed like Luke might be able to.

Luke finally woke about an hour after Theo. He grunted, and flopped onto his back. It was still barely light outside, but the curtains weren't completely shut, so there was just enough grey morning light for Theo to see as Luke cranked his eyes open and smiled sleepily.

"Morning," Luke croaked, then cleared his throat and managed more clearly, "How are you, did you sleep okay?"

"I'm good, and yeah. I slept fine. How about you?"

"Like a baby." Luke put a hand on Theo's shoulder and stroked up to his neck and back down, leaving a tingling trail with the touch of his hand.

Theo laughed. "Most babies wake every few hours, so I've never understood that simile."

"Huh. Yeah. Good point. Like a log then."

Theo leaned over and kissed Luke's cheek. "Now you're awake, I need to go for a piss. I didn't want to disturb you." He slipped out of bed and shivered as the cold air hit his skin. "Fuck, it's chilly out here."

"There's a robe on the back of the door."

Theo found it, and wrapped it around himself. It smelled of Luke. "Thanks."

"What time do you need to leave to get back for Archie?" Luke craned his head up to look at the digital clock by the bed. It was just after half eight.

"In an hour, or even less would be good so I can shower and change."

"No worries. We can go soon. I'll get the kettle on and see what there is for breakfast. Are you a morning tea or coffee guy?"

"Tea please."

THEY MADE it over to Theo's in plenty of time.

"So, this is my place." Theo took Luke's jacket and hung it up in the hall, then showed him into the living room. "Feel free to nose around and help yourself to a drink or something. Make yourself at home."

When he came back ten minutes later, clean and wearing fresh clothes, he was amused to find Luke sitting cross-legged on the living room floor playing with Archie's Lego.

"What are you making?" He came to sit beside him.

"A castle," Luke replied, tearing his focus away for a moment to give Theo a grin. "Wanna help? I fucking love Lego. I was gutted when my mum gave all mine away without asking me. I should have taken it with me when I left home."

"Sure." Theo scooped up a handful of bricks and joined in the construction.

They were so absorbed, they lost track of time and it

was only when the doorbell rang that Theo realised how late it was.

"That'll be Archie and Caroline. Do you want to meet her?" Caroline would be surprised to find that Theo had company, but she'd be happy about him dating someone and he was sure she'd like Luke.

Luke frowned. "I would like to meet her if you're okay with that. But what about the Santa plan? Won't Archie be suspicious if he sees me, then Santa, then me again?"

"Hmm, yeah. Good point. I don't want to ruin the magic for him yet. You can meet Caroline another time." It was only after saying the words that Theo realised it sounded a little presumptuous.

But Luke just nodded. "Sure."

"Okay. You go and hide in my room and get the suit on while I answer the door. Once Caroline's gone, I'll distract Archie with his presents under the tree—and you can sneak out and ring the doorbell from outside."

Theo and Caroline exchanged a quick hug in greeting on the doorstep. She was on her way to work so Theo didn't invite her in.

"Did you have a nice Christmas?" Theo asked.

"Yes, lovely thanks. You?"

"Yes, it was really good in the end." Theo's sappy smile must have given him away, because Caroline narrowed her eyes and grinned.

"Oh yes? Did you have company?"

Theo nodded and flushed.

"New boyfriend?"

Theo shrugged, aware that Luke might be listening in to this. "Maybe."

"It is Luke?" Archie piped up. "I like Luke. He's nice. And he's friends with Santa."

Caroline arched her eyebrows. "I see I have some gossip to catch up on. But sadly I have to dash or I'll be late. You can fill me in another time."

Once she was gone, Theo took Archie's overnight bag. "I'll go and put this in your room. Why don't you go and play in the living room for a minute."

"Have I got Christmas presents?" Archie asked hopefully.

"Of course," Theo said. "They're under the tree, but wait for me to get back before you open them."

When Archie hurried into the living room, Theo dumped his bag in his room, and then quickly nipped into his own bedroom to see Luke dressed in full Santa regalia, apart from his beard which was still in his hand. "Do you need a present to give him?" Theo asked. "He'll be expecting one I think. I can get one of the smaller ones I bought him."

"I came prepared." Luke turned, smiling. He pointed to the bed where there was a small, wrapped parcel waiting. "I think he'll approve."

Warmth spread through Theo's chest at Luke's thoughtfulness. Archie was going to be so excited. "You're the best," he said.

"Glad you think so."

"Right, I'll keep Archie busy while you finish up."

Archie was absorbed with the Lego when Theo went back into the living room, his presents still sat under the tree untouched. The castle was the perfect distraction.

"This is a good castle." He added a brick to a tower at one end. "I'm making this bit even taller."

"Yeah?" Theo joined him on the floor. "Cool. So, are you ready to open some presents now, Archie?"

The ones under the tree were from Theo, and there

were also ones that Theo's parents had sent in the post. It wasn't a huge pile, but he'd already had lots yesterday of course.

"Yes!" Archie's eyes lit up. He crawled over to the tree and predictably pulled out the biggest one first, which was his main present, a remote-control car.

It didn't take him long to work his way through the gifts under the tree, but he was thrilled with each of them: some more Lego, some colouring pencils, cuddly toys, and some story books. With perfect timing, as the wrapping came off the last present—some additions to his wooden train set from Theo's mum and dad—the doorbell rang.

"Oh. I wonder who that could be," Theo said, getting up. "Do you want to come and see, Archie?"

"Okay." Archie hopped up and followed Theo to the front door.

As Theo opened it, he wished he could see the expression on Archie's face. But his surprised gasp and cry of, "Santa! Daddy, it's Santa!" was enough.

Luke stood there on the doorstep, sticking out his fake belly as he said in his jolliest Santa voice, "Well, hello, Archie. How are you today?" He had a bag in his hand—actually, it was one of Theo's pillowcases, acting as an impromptu Santa sack. Theo hid his chuckle when he noticed.

"I'm very well thank you. I got more presents, and my daddy made a Lego castle, and I got a remote-control car and lots of things."

"Can I come in and see?"

"Yes." Archie took Luke's hand and led him into the living room, leaving Theo to close the front door.

"You sit there." Archie guided Luke to the sofa and proceeded to bring all his presents one at a time for Luke's inspection. Only after he'd showed him the last one, did he seem to notice that Luke had something with him.

"Is that for me?" he asked.

"It sure is. I couldn't visit you and not bring you one more present." Luke held the pillowcase open so Archie could reach inside and pull out the gift.

"Thank you," Archie said as he tore into the wrapping. "Oh, look!" He held up a yellow dog with floppy ears. "This one can be Mr Yellow. He needs to meet my other Santa toys. Where's my bag, Daddy?"

"In your room, Arch."

Mr Yellow in hand, Archie hurried off.

"He's so cute," Luke said quietly in his normal voice when Archie was gone.

"Yeah?" Theo said, heart swelling.

Luke grinned, mostly hidden by his beard, but his eyes were full of warmth as he said, "Yeah. Figures though. His dad's cute too."

Theo beamed, hopelessly smitten.

"Look!" Archie was back, his arms full of his animals from Santa. He lined them up on the sofa next to Luke. "Mr Purple, Mrs Blue, Mr Green, and Mr Yellow. Mr Purple is my favourite because I had him first."

"Well I'm very glad you like them, Archie," Luke said. "I think they have found a very happy home with you." He stood, patting his belly. "I have to go now. It's been a busy month and I need a rest before I start getting ready for next Christmas."

"Okay," Archie said. "Bye, Santa."

"Bye, Archie. See you next year."

Theo saw "Santa" out and gave Luke his car key on the doorstep. "Leave the suit in the boot of my car," he whispered. "We can rescue it later."

When the doorbell rang again five minutes later, Archie looked up from the train set he was building around the Lego castle. "Who's that now?"

"Let's see, shall we?"

Archie's happy, "Hello Luke!" was almost as warm a greeting as Luke had got in Santa mode and it made Theo smile. Archie ushered him into the living room to show him his presents, and the fact that Luke had bought him another present—an animal jigsaw puzzle—meant that Archie was on cloud nine.

"It's got a monkey in it, like Mr Green. And an elephant like Mr Purple!" He pointed to the picture on the outside of the box. "Will you help me do it, Luke?"

"Sure."

Luke sat on the sofa and helped Archie do the puzzle on the coffee table while Theo went to make them some tea. When Theo came back they were engrossed. He paused in the doorway for a moment, heart warmed by the sight of his son with Luke.

"Maybe try turning that one around, mate," Luke said, as Archie tried to fit a piece into the puzzle.

"Like that?" Archie had another try. "Yes! It fits!" He went back to the pieces that were spread out on the table. "Oh look. I've found another edge piece."

Theo came to sit beside Luke and handed him a mug of tea. "Looks like you're doing a great job with the puzzle, Archie."

"Luke, can you find me some more bits of elephant?" Archie asked.

Luke put his tea down out of Archie's reach, and skimmed the pieces carefully, picking out a few bits with grey on. "Here you go."

He was great with Archie, patient, and giving him just

enough help to keep him engaged, but not taking over like some adults did when they played with kids. Archie responded to him, listening to his suggestions. When he finally put the last piece into place he beamed at Luke. "We did it!"

"High five." Luke held up his hand for Archie to slap.

"Will you read me a story now?" Archie asked. "I got some new ones from my daddy."

Luke glanced at Theo and raised his eyebrows. "If that's okay with your dad? He might want to read them to you himself."

Theo smiled and shook his head. "It's fine." He was glad to see Archie and Luke bonding. "I need to go and start making some soup for lunch anyway." He picked up his now-empty mug and stood. "I'll leave you guys to it."

BY THE TIME lunch was ready, Luke and Archie had worked their way through all Archie's new stories, and were back on the floor playing with the Lego and the trains. Theo came to tell them that the soup was on the table, and he could hardly get through the door of the living room because the whole floor was covered with train track, Lego structures, and plastic animals.

"Wow. You've been busy. How's the castle coming along?"

"It's not a castle anymore," Archie informed him. "It's a zoo, with a train that takes the people around to see all the animals."

"Cool." Theo was impressed. It was pretty awesome. "Lunch is ready now though, so can you come to the table?"

"But I'm not hungry." Archie went back to linking pieces of track. "Don't want lunch."

"Come on, Arch. It's lunchtime now, and it's ready and waiting," Theo said.

"Nooo." Archie's voice took on a familiar whiny tone.

Theo was about to use his firm voice, and maybe even use the old counting-to-five trick, when Luke got there first, standing up and saying, "I'm really hungry. What are we having?"

"Leek and potato soup and cheese on toast," Theo said.

"Oh wow, that sounds yummy. Are you coming, Archie? We can finish this after." Luke held out his hand.

Archie looked up, and Theo could see him warring between staying and playing, or coming with Luke who was his new favourite person. "Yeah, okay," he finally said, putting down the train he was holding and standing up and taking Luke's hand.

As they walked into the kitchen, Luke winked at Theo.

"Thanks," Theo mouthed over Archie's head, grinning.

When they'd finished eating, Archie asked if he could get down to play again.

"Sure, wipe your fingers on the cloth by the sink first though, they're all greasy from the cheese."

Archie obliged. "You coming to help with the zoo, Luke?"

"I'll be there in a little while. I'm going to help your dad clear up first."

"Okay." Off he trotted.

"You're popular," Theo said once Archie had gone. "Definitely a hit with him."

Luke flushed, but he looked pleased. "He's a great kid."

"Yeah," Theo smiled proudly. "Yeah, he is."

They cleared the table, and Theo stacked the dishwasher while Luke helped carry things over. Then Luke washed up the soup pan while Theo leaned back against the kitchen counter watching him. He couldn't hold back his smile.

"What are you grinning at?" Luke asked as he drained the water.

"Just you in my kitchen. I like seeing you here."

"I like being in your kitchen." Luke advanced on Theo with a predatory gleam in his eyes that made Theo feel hot all over. The morning had been very chaste with the focus on Archie. But now they were momentarily alone, Theo's mind went back to the amazing sex they'd had yesterday and he tingled with expectation as Luke closed in on him and stepped between Theo's thighs.

Theo slipped his arms around Luke's shoulders as Luke gripped his hips with firm hands. When their lips finally met in a kiss, it was deep and sensual, their tongues touching and sliding as they tasted each other.

Luke was the first to pull back, and Theo tried to stop him, curling a hand around his nape to keep him close.

"Time out," Luke murmured, leaning his forehead on Theo's. "If you carry on kissing me like that it will only get harder to stop."

"Yeah," Theo agreed regretfully, bringing his hand to Luke's cheek instead, enjoying the sensation of Luke's beard against his palm. He pressed a gentle, closed-mouth kiss to Luke's lips instead. "You're right." Another kiss.

"Are you Daddy's boyfriend, Luke?" Archie's voice from the kitchen doorway had Luke pulling back abruptly, looking as guilty as a kid who'd been caught with his hand in the cookie jar.

"Um." Luke looked at Archie, then back at Theo with a slightly panicked expression on his face. He raised his eyebrows in a *what the fuck do I say to that?* kind of way.

"Yes," Theo said. "Yes, Arch. Luke's my boyfriend."

Luke stared at Theo in shock and Theo stared back. His heart thumped wildly, hoping he'd read the situation right. After what felt like forever, but was probably a matter of seconds, Luke's face slowly morphed from shock into a grin that made Theo's stomach explode with butterflies. "Yeah," he voiced his agreement. "I am your daddy's boyfriend. I hope that's okay." Breaking their gaze, he turned to Archie who was studying them as if they were animals in the zoo.

"Yes," Archie said. "My mummy has a boyfriend too. He's called Daniel. Will you come and play with the zoo again now, Luke?"

"I'll be there in a minute, Archie," Luke said. "You go and get out some more animals, okay?"

"Okay."

When Archie was gone, Luke said, "So. Are we really? Boyfriends?"

"If you want?" A jolt of uncertainty sent an icicle into Theo's gut. Had he pushed Luke into it? Had he made a mistake?

But Luke smiled. "Yes. I want. I really want." He moved in close to Theo again, hands back on his hips and Theo waited for the kiss he knew was coming. Then Luke added, "I didn't know I was going to get a new boyfriend for Christmas. But if I'd written a list for Santa this year it would definitely have been at the top."

Theo chuckled. "Yeah, same. I guess we must have both been very good to deserve this."

"I guess we must." Luke kissed him at last, sweet and certain, and full of promise, and Theo kissed him back.

EPILOGUE

Almost one year later

"HI, LUKE." Caroline smiled as she opened the door to him. She pulled him into a hug and kissed his cheek, her pregnant belly nudging against him. "Come in for a minute. Archie's still deciding which toys to bring."

"How are you?" he asked as he followed her into the living room. A brightly lit Christmas tree stood in the bay window, haphazardly covered in fairy lights, tinsel, and decorations—including some obviously made by Archie at school. Theo and Luke had similar ones on their tree. Luke had moved into Theo's flat back in August and he was used to thinking of it as home now.

"Exhausted, I could have done without a block of night shifts this week, but I'm surviving. I can't wait to start maternity leave at the end of next week."

"I bet."

Caroline looked tired. Radiant but wilting a little, like a rose that was starting to fade. She eased her bulk down onto the sofa and sat with a hand on her stomach. "Oh, she's kicking me again."

Luke chuckled. "That must be so weird."

"It really is. I don't think I'll ever get used to it. Do you want to feel?"

"Okay." A bit self-conscious, yet fascinated, Luke moved to sit close beside her and offered his hand. He remembered doing this with his sister when she was pregnant, and he'd found it equally hard then to equate the bump to a baby.

She took it and placed it on her belly. It was solid, like a drum skin stretched tight, and as Luke's hand rested there he felt a nudge against his palm, followed by another more definite poke. "Wow!" He chuckled as he took his hand back. "She's strong."

"She is."

Daniel came in with Archie's overnight bag in one hand and Archie's backpack in the other. "Hi, Luke."

Luke gave him a nod and a smile in greeting.

"Hello, Luke!" Archie exploded into the room in a burst of energy and enthusiasm. "High five."

"Hey, buddy." Luke offered a hand to Archie who slapped it, and then climbed onto the sofa and gave Luke a hug for good measure.

"What are we going to do today, Luke? Can we go on the train like Daddy said last week?"

"I think your dad said maybe, Archie. But yeah, we'll go on the train. Your dad's working till three so we can head to the mall after lunch and go on the train, and then give him a lift home after."

"Yay!" Archie bounced on the sofa and clapped his hands. "And can we go and see Santa too? I haven't seen him yet this year. Will at school says Santa isn't real, but I think he is. Because I met him last year. He came to my house and everything."

Luke exchanged covert grins with Caroline and Daniel who knew all about Luke's Santa secret. "Yes, definitely. We can do that while we're there today."

"I can bring Mr Purple to see him, to show that I've looked after him for a whole year."

"Good plan." Mr Purple was still one of Archie's favourite toys. He always took him back and forth between his two homes and he was in Archie's bed every night. When Archie had started primary school in September, they'd had a job persuading him to leave Mr Purple at home every day after being allowed to have him at nursery. "Okay, Archie, are you ready to go?"

"Yes." Archie jumped off the sofa and landed with a thud. He took his little rucksack from Daniel.

"Enjoy the peace and quiet," Luke said with a wink to Caroline. He leaned over to kiss her cheek.

"I will. I think I'm going back to bed for a nap."

"Sounds like a plan." Luke stood up and took Archie's other bag from Daniel. "Cheers."

"See you, man." Daniel clapped him on the shoulder. "Have fun with Archie."

"Oh, we will. Say goodbye now, Archie, and we'll head off."

Archie ran over to hug and kiss Caroline, and then Daniel—who crouched down to hug him and ruffle his hair. "Bye, Mummy; bye, Daniel. Come on, Luke!"

THE MALL WAS PREDICTABLY CROWDED for a Saturday before Christmas. It made Luke glad that he'd been transferred to a pharmacy in the city instead. The decorations were amazing though, and Luke paused to tilt his head back and admire them. He hadn't been out here since they went up this season. They'd gone with a red and silver theme this year and strings of red baubles and silver stars hung from the high glass ceilings, glittering where the light caught them.

"Luke, Luke, look at the Christmas tree!" Archie was tugging on his hand to get his attention, and he pulled Luke through the throngs of shoppers to get close to the giant tree in the middle of the shopping centre. It was a real one, huge and imposing, and festooned with twinkling lights and strings of silver and red tinsel, interspersed with decorations. Luke's lips twitched in amusement when he noticed what was hanging on the tree: hundreds of red and white candy canes. He was surprised Theo hadn't mentioned it. Maybe he hadn't paused to look on his way back and forth to work. Usually rushing to arrive and leave, he probably hadn't paid attention to the detail.

Luke got his phone out and opened WhatsApp. He snapped a quick photo of the tree and added the caption: *Look closely, remind you of something lurking at the back of your underwear drawer? We should dig it out soon. Tis the season... ;)*

He pressed send, knowing Theo wouldn't see it till he finished his shift. But hopefully it would make him smile. Then he added:

I'm here with Archie by the way. We're going on the train, and he wants to see Santa later. Msg me when you're free and you can come and find us and I'll give you a lift home.

They shared Theo's car now, and he'd got the bus into work so Luke had the car to get around with Archie.

"Right, Archie. Let's go and ride on the train. Then we can go and book you in to visit Santa after lunch."

SANTA WAS IN DEMAND TODAY, so they couldn't get in to see him till the 4pm slot. By that time, Theo had come to find them, so they all went into the grotto together each holding one of Archie's hands as they entered. Luke noticed a few people glancing their way and taking in their family set-up. Luke didn't care. He was proud to be seen with Theo and Archie.

Archie made his way to the table where paper and crayons were set out, and started drawing while they were waiting for his number to be called. Theo and Luke found a couple of adult-sized chairs and sat down with other parents. A dad was checking his phone, and a mum was breastfeeding a baby.

"Hello!" A familiar voice made Luke look up to see Jamie—clad in all his elfish finery. "Fancy seeing you here. What brings you back? Couldn't stay away?"

"Hey, Jamie." Luke stood and gave him a quick hug. "I didn't know you were working here again this year."

"Yeah, well." Jamie shrugged. "The money's not bad." He lowered his voice. "And between you and me, my arse looks pretty good in these britches. I used the uniform in my current Grindr profile pic and I've had more messages this week than I've had in the last month. Who knew elf kink was a thing?"

Luke laughed. "Oh my God, Jamie. Only you." He glanced over to where Archie was busy colouring. "So, yeah. I'm here with Theo, my partner. Theo, this is Jamie —" Theo got up and shook Jamie's hand "—and Archie, over there at the drawing table." Then it was his turn to lower his voice. "I don't know if you remember them visiting Santa last year? But Archie doesn't know that I used to work here, and he still thinks Santa's real, so...."

"Oh that's awesome." Jamie grinned. "Look at you three, all happy families. How cute."

Luke grinned, a pleased flush heating his cheeks as he took Theo's hand where Theo stood beside him. "Yeah. It's pretty good."

"And don't worry. Your Santa secret is safe with me." Jamie mimed zipping his lips. "Okay, I'd better get back to my elf duties. I'll see you when your number comes up."

Jamie trotted off, and Luke kept hold of Theo's hand as they sat back down.

Theo chuckled. "Santa secret, sounds mysterious."

"Maybe my official title should be Secret Santa. Makes me sound like James Bond or something."

Theo snorted. "In your dreams. You're not cool enough to be James Bond."

Luke turned to him in mock outrage. "Hurtful!"

"But Secret Santa is more my cup of tea anyway, especially when he brings me presents like the one I got last year." Theo grinned, and Luke was helpless to do anything but smile back.

"Love you," he whispered so only Theo could hear him.

Theo squeezed his hand. "Love you too."

ABOUT THE AUTHOR

Jay lives just outside Bristol in the West of England. He comes from a family of writers, but always used to believe that the gene for fiction writing had passed him by. He spent years only ever writing emails, articles, or website content.

One day, Jay decided to try and write a short story—just to see if he could—and found it rather addictive. He hasn't stopped writing since.

Jay is transgender and was formerly known as she/her.

www.jaynorthcote.com
Twitter: @Jay_Northcote
Facebook: Jay Northcote Fiction

MORE FROM JAY NORTHCOTE

The Law of Attraction
Imperfect Harmony
Into You
Cold Feet
What Happens at Christmas
A Family for Christmas
Summer Heat
Tops Down Bottoms Up
The Half Wolf

Printed in Poland
by Amazon Fulfillment
Poland Sp. z o.o., Wrocław

50547895R00089